MW01147381

All That Survives
A Post-Apocalyptic EMP Survival Thriller

JACK HUNT

DIRECT RESPONSE PUBLISHING

ISBN: 9781689254014

Also By Jack Hunt

The Renegades
The Renegades 2: Aftermath
The Renegades 3: Fortress
The Renegades 4: Colony
The Renegades 5: United
Mavericks: Hunters Moon
Killing Time
State of Panic
State of Shock
State of Decay
Defiant
Phobia
Anxiety
Strain
Blackout
Darkest Hour
Final Impact
And Many More…

Dedication

For my family.

Prologue

Joanna Camlin hadn't come here expecting to die.

The maniac pulled tight on the rope with a crazed look in his eye. Was this how it would end? Her father had warned her of the dangers of hiking the Appalachian Trail, and that was long before the event. The event that had stripped the nation of power and crippled the infrastructure. The event that had forced people to commit all kinds of atrocities in order to survive. The event that had kept her away from towns, thinking it was safer in the wilderness. She wished she'd listened to him. But at twenty-one, she was impulsive, hungry for adventure, and not even wild horses could have dragged her away.

Now had he asked her when she was fifteen, in high school, and a Girl Scout, she may have agreed. Back then her love of the outdoors was marred by unrealistic expectations, a one-time brush with poison oak and an unhealthy fear of bugs. Of course she got over that but not the memory. She could still recall the itching and throbbing blisters after hiking miles into Yosemite National Park on a trail no more than two feet wide.

It was then she'd heard of the Appalachian Trail, or simply the AT as it was known. The AT was considered the granddaddy of all long-distance wilderness trails in the USA. Extending from Georgia to Maine, it attracted thousands every year. Her scout leader had talked about it with such fondness as if it was the last true adventure. That had stuck with her. Joanna remembered her face lighting up as she pulled out a map and ran a finger over a red line that covered over 2,000 miles, fourteen states and a variety of elevations that went as high as 6,000 feet.

But it wasn't all wilderness and mountain ridges; it

crossed fields, highways and towns, many of which were only a few miles from the path drawing in hikers and backpackers attempting to hike it all in a single season. Maybe that's what piqued her fascination. Or perhaps at the age of twenty-one, after finishing college, she simply refused to fall into the trap of spending the next forty years of her life tangled up in excuses and some job she hated only to accept adventure as a limited week long vacation.

Go to college, get a job, get married, have kids and die.

Nope. Not her. Not yet. She was young, fearless and free and there was plenty of time for that kind of ankle-weight behavior. *Oh God, why hadn't she listened?*

The rope dug deep into her throat, a painful twist of fate that not even she could have foreseen. She screamed in agony; her cries lost in the darkness of the woodland.

If only they'd stayed in one of the towns they'd passed through on their way south from Maine. Would they have encountered others like him? Desperate people, changed by the event. Was that what had caused him to lose his mind?

Even as he continued his tirade of strangulation, she questioned it all.

The breakdown hadn't occurred all at once nor were all the towns across America affected the same way. Some fared well, rallying together, protecting their own, while others simply fell apart.

In the beginning the reports of chaos sweeping the nation, mass looting and confusion were rampant. Cities were the first to suffer, many destroyed in hours as planes crashed to the earth tearing through homes and businesses, and reducing entire communities to rubble. The power outages, loss of water, lack of communication and end of transportation presented a challenge that was far too great for government and emergency services to handle.

Days turned to weeks, weeks to months and disarray soon became the norm.

Already hiking the trail at the time, Joanna thought they'd find safety in the wilderness of the Appalachian

Mountains.

How wrong she was.

Traveling with her boyfriend Luke, and three close friends, Michaela, Hilary and Chris, she couldn't have imagined anything going wrong. Chris had already hiked the trail once in his life, and Luke had a career as a police officer. They were armed and more than ready to deal with trouble, until trouble changed all that.

Somewhere in the George Washington National Forest, they'd come across an oddball that went by the trail name, Maestro. He was a hippie-looking fella in his late twenties, carrying a banjo and looking as if he had consumed one too many magic mushrooms. He'd stopped by their camp and asked for a cigarette but none of them smoked. He'd continued on his way only to spook Michaela an hour later while she was cleaning herself in a river nearby.

She'd managed to collect her clothes and Luke and Chris went to check it out but by then he was gone. That had been in the afternoon.

After they retired to their tents for the evening, Joanna had heard someone rooting through the campsite. At first she thought it was a bear but then she heard a voice.

"Luke. Luke, wake up," she said shaking him.

He rolled her way. "What's the matter?" he asked groggily.

"Someone's out there. I think it's that guy."

"Ah, it's nothing. Go back to sleep."

"Luke."

Before he could crawl out of his sleeping bag, she heard liquid being splashed, then a whoosh before a glow of light followed by Michaela and Hilary screaming.

They scrambled out.

Joanna could smell the blaze before she saw it, the smoke wafting over. Shouting and screams mixed together as she turned to see Chris and Michaela's tent on fire and the same man nearby holding a gasoline can in one hand, and a gun in the other.

They were trapped inside. Even as a hole appeared in the tent and Michaela stumbled out, the man shot her in the back three times then looked over at them.

"Run," Luke said to her as he tackled the lunatic to the ground.

Joanna looked over her shoulder as she ran, then tripped on a large tree root. Her knees ground into the earth causing her to scream in pain. Behind her Luke was rolling on the ground with their attacker while Michaela lay motionless only a few feet away.

Staggering to her feet, she was torn between running and going back to help but it was the sight of the man shooting Luke in the stomach twice then looking her way that made her bolt. Her thighs burned as she barreled through the blackness of night, trees exploding into view. Her foot caught again and this time she rolled down a steep embankment, coming to a stop as she collided with a tree. She lay there for a minute or two before looking up and seeing the hippie pitch sideways and make his way down.

Up and running again, tears streaming down her face, she regretted not listening to her father. If she'd stayed in

New York she might have got into trouble but at least she would have been relatively safe, surrounded by family. Now there was no one. No one to hear her cries. No one to prevent the rope from going around her neck.

Taken down, like a lion on a gazelle, she thrashed in the man's grasp, begging, pleading for her life but that only seemed to excite him more. She scratched his face in one final attempt to claw at his eyes only to be punched so hard she lost consciousness.

She came to as the rope bit into her neck.

Drained of strength to fight she looked at her attacker through tears, hoping her face might invoke sympathy and somehow stop the madness, but it didn't. He continued his tirade of violence. She gagged and coughed.

Gasping for air, on the verge of blacking out she went limp, hoping that might give her a chance.

It didn't.

She succumbed to the nothingness of death just as he walked away playing a sickening tune on his banjo.

Chapter 1

Destination: Damascus, Virginia

Approximate time: 10:05 a.m.

The nearby echo of a gun put them on high alert.

Trouble was expected; it was a way of life now that it had been almost four months since the blackout. Only Beth knew the degree of danger lurking beyond Pisgah National Forest, as Landon had spent the better part of three months laid up in bed, resting his legs and trying to come to terms with a world without power, the plane crash, the death of his daughter and killing a man after the run-in with Cayden.

In that time not a day had passed he hadn't thought of home.

He was desperate to see Sara and Max and yet worried sick at her reaction to the news that Ellie was dead. He'd have to relive it all again, and watch them suffer through the grief. It was pain he wouldn't wish upon anyone, certainly not his family.

But he had to get home. He had to protect them.

Had Castine gone the way of Ryerson? Based on the little Beth had said, Ryerson had collapsed within a matter of a month. Looting. Desperation. Hunger. Disease. Ignorance on how to survive. All of it led to civil unrest and with it, people taking matters into their own hands.

They could have survived together up on that mountain but for how long?

With uncertainty looming on the horizon, conversation soon turned to leaving.

What were the options?

What was it like out there?

Although Beth had been adamant in December about staying, four months had given her plenty of time to reconsider. It probably helped that he'd said it would be a shame not to hike the AT. Eventually she agreed. "Let's get something straight, I'm not going to Maine because I want to, or need you, okay? I just think you don't know the first damn thing about surviving out there and I can't have that on my conscience, especially not after all the work I've gone through to get you back on your feet again," she'd said.

Landon stifled a laugh and nodded. "A lot of work for nothing."

"Yeah. Now whether I'll stay when I arrive is another thing entirely."

"Of course." He smiled back and she narrowed her gaze and jabbed a finger at him.

He played along with it, letting her think that was the case. But even if she wasn't willing to admit it, they'd grown fond of each other's company in the short time and had become dependent on each other. Him, more so than her. In many ways he was indebted to her for saving his life. Had she not shown up that wintry night in December, he would have died out there alongside Dustin and Ellie.

In the months after, his grief had almost destroyed him. There were moments he wanted to die if only to escape the misery of his thoughts. It didn't help that there had been nights he'd seen Ellie in his dreams. She'd come to him to say that she was okay. It seemed as real as his waking state. But he wasn't sure if it was real or just his mind trying to cope with survivor's guilt. Why had he survived and she hadn't? She had her whole life ahead of her. She hadn't wronged anyone. It just didn't make sense.

As for Beth's grief? Well, she had gone through hell too. He'd heard her sobbing into her pillow every night for several months. She must have thought he couldn't hear because by morning she would act as if she was fine but he knew the truth. A few times he'd tried to talk about it but she shifted the topic. She was good at that. Other times she came up with reasons to avoid discussing her parents. Landon never pushed it. He figured she'd eventually open up.

"So when are we leaving?" he'd asked.

"The end of April — to avoid winter. The weather will be better. Though the nights will be chilly, probably dipping into the low thirties, but I've packed accordingly."

And pack she had. Her father had been an outdoor education director, and in preparation to hike the AT together, they'd already gathered an arsenal of gear — though she did have to do another run into town to collect more in the first few weeks after the blackout.

In the evenings, snowed in, Beth had given him a crash course in the kinds of dangers they would face on the trail, how it would affect them physically and mentally, and what it would take to survive outside. He thought it was as simple as having a backpack, a shelter, something to eat and drink and a sturdy pair of hiking boots.

Nope. For the stretch of terrain they were about to embark on, it relied on much more. They would require specific foods that provided a good combination of fats, carbs and proteins and could last for 3 to 4 days. Gear needed to be lightweight, preferably under 20 pounds.

They also needed 1 to 2 liters of water, plus ways of purifying it, cooking food, and staying warm and dry to avoid hypothermia. Resupplies were usually picked up in designated communities along the AT; Damascus would be the first stop for them.

"Late April but I thought you said the end of March?"

"No, the doc said three months minimum. But I want to make sure you're ready. I can't have you slowing me down," she said.

"Because you're in that much of a hurry to make it there?"

"No. I just…" She realized what she'd said and went back to preparing the gear. "All right, let's go over this."

She'd laid everything out and had been through it countless times because she was sure she'd forget something. "Two Osprey Atmos AG 65 backpacks, two REI Co-op Magma 15 sleeping bags."

"Check," he said, checking the list almost with his eyes closed.

"Two 10-liter dry bags for the sleeping bags."

"Check."

"An MSR pocket rocket stove."

"Check."

"Two Platypus gravity filters, a life straw and some Aquaria water drops."

"Check. C'mon, Beth, we've been through this enough times."

"Just one last time."

And it went on like that through a list of headlamps, hiking poles, tent, fire starters, bear bag, food, weapons and so on.

While the majority of thru-hikers began the northbound trek of the AT in late March to mid-April in order to avoid a time crunch and make it to Katahdin before Baxter State Park closed in October, they didn't have that concern. It was more about making sure Landon's legs were healed enough to handle the rigorous hike.

As they would be hiking roughly sixteen miles a day with a few twenty to twenty-five mile days, he knew it was better to wait a little longer than find himself unable to make the journey that would take at least three months to complete based on their current location.

Three months. He couldn't believe it would take that long before he could see his family. A lot of shit could happen on the trail, but he had to put that out of his mind. It was too overwhelming.

First step. Reach Damascus.

But it wasn't far from there that the problems began.

With over fifty miles to cover, and roughly nineteen hours until reaching their first stop in the small town of Damascus, Virginia, Landon had already worked up a sweat that drenched his shirt. Twenty pounds didn't seem like a lot when he saw it on the ground but after strapping on his backpack and walking just an hour, his heart was pounding and his thighs burned.

He dug the walking sticks into the spring earth, remembering that their goal was to walk at least sixteen miles a day. Sixteen? He was ready to give up after just eight miles. Beth took the lead scanning for threats with

Grizzly at the rear. She'd already warned him that it wasn't going to be easy. It wasn't just a simple straight path to Maine. No, the Appalachian mountain range had some of the most grueling terrain in the USA. They would traverse well-worn trails that curved wildly, over rocks, up and down mountains, through valleys and across fields and roads. The path known to many as the green tunnel due to the tree cover most of the way wasn't for the faint of heart. Many who embarked each year never finished, and those hikers weren't facing the horrors of a nation without power. There was no way of knowing what they would encounter, but hell or high water, Landon was going to complete the journey.

In order to join the trail in Damascus, the initial chunk of their trip involved trudging through the Cherokee National Forest, crossing over into Tennessee and going through a few tiny communities like Beech Creek, Neva, Mountain City and Laurel Bloomery.

It was in those first few hours they encountered the first hurdle just on the outskirts of Beech Creek.

"Look at those bastards. Everyone wants to take what another has," Landon whispered. "We should help them."

Beth shook her head. "There will be a lot of people out here like this. We can't help everyone. No, we'll go around."

She was dressed in tight faded jeans, a warm navy blue hooded winter coat and a beanie hat pulled down over her long blond hair. Both of them wore layers as temperatures would vary from day to day and they needed to be able to adapt to the ever-changing weather conditions. Rain, heat, wind, snow, it was all so unpredictable. What they wore could either be their enemy or savior from blistering heat or chilly nights. He was wearing Buff Headwear, a long-sleeve compression shirt, hiking pants and trail runners.

Beth was prone and staring through the scope on a Howa Mini Action .300 BLK. That damn thing only weighed 6 pounds and had enough punch to drop a deer from 200 yards out.

Beth was different from Ellie in so many ways. Ellie

was confident but a real girls' girl. At only eighteen, Beth was mature beyond her years, carrying herself with the confidence of someone who'd lived thirty years.

They'd taken the rifle off one of Cayden's guys after the assault. He'd had a hard time believing she'd taken out all four but when she explained it, it seemed to make sense. Rhett had done a fine job of raising her to be self-reliant, confident and situationally aware. A week after the assault, Landon had asked her if she wanted to talk about it. She'd been quiet but he'd come to realize that was just her. She wasn't loud or brash, seeking attention like some young girls or boasting about what she knew about survival. There was a depth to her that he'd only just begun to see.

Beth popped up from a prone position, ready to leave. Landon followed but the cries of a young girl reached him and he couldn't bring himself to walk away. "Just let me take a look," he said.

"Landon. You want to reach Maine. We've got a lot of miles to cover. We can't just stop every day for someone who's caught up in some unfortunate situation."

"No? Is that what you thought when you saw the plane come down?"

"That was different."

"Just let me take a look."

She groaned and handed him a pair of compact binoculars. He peered through and scanned. "There's three of them," he said. "They've dragged the mother and father outside, and now they've got a girl." He glanced up at Beth. "She can't be older than eight." It was strange to think he needed her permission to help as he was older than her. Had it been Ellie he would have made the call but he trusted Beth's expertise. Heck, she'd kept him alive this long. He looked back through the binos. The three dirty men looked like they hadn't taken a bath in months. Their faces were covered in dirt, and their clothes ratty as if they'd torn them in the brush.

Landon was hidden by the thick foliage and trees that hedged in the road they were traveling on. It was a rural area with homes spread out along a large double-lane road that cut through the heart of the town. Many of the homes had been ransacked or burnt to the ground. Broken windows, and furniture dragged out onto lawns near the dead, revealed the sign of the times.

With enough supplies for the next four days they didn't bother venturing into homes. There was no need, at least not yet. Besides, walking into one with a scared family could mean eating lead for supper. No, they needed to remain calm, cautious and avoid trouble.

Except trouble was everywhere.

After a gunshot, they'd heard cries and taken cover. Avoidance was the best tactic, not being a hero, but there were only three of them. A clean shot from Beth, and he figured he could take one out. The other one would likely turn and run. With the coverage of trees, the assailants wouldn't even know where they were. In his mind the risk factor was low. He shared his idea.

"Beth, we can walk on but who knows what they'll do."

Beth sighed and ran a hand over her face.

ALL THAT SURVIVES: A Post-Apocalyptic EMP Survival Thriller

A bead of sweat formed on his brow and ran down his temple. He wiped it with the back of his arm and took another look while Beth did the same. "No. If that third one doesn't bolt, they could still wind up dead. He could grab the kid and barricade himself in the house. Then what?"

"So I take out the one closest to the kid. You know how this is going to end if we don't intervene. Alternatively I can try to talk them down from the ledge," he said with an amused smile knowing full well that they were far beyond that point. Negotiations were a thing of the past. The only thing people understood now was the bullet.

"But you'd need to get closer. That shotgun won't cut it from here."

He was carrying a Mossberg 500 courtesy of Cayden. He glanced at it.

"Yeah," she said. "What you see and what I see are two different things."

She was right. He hadn't thought it through.

"What if I draw one of them away?"

She frowned. "You'll only make the other two nervous — again not a good situation. No, we move on. It's too risky." She stared at him for a few seconds and he realized she was right. "Let's go, Grizzly," she said leading the way. Under his breath he apologized as if he was responsible for their well-being. Even as he looked back at the family and placed himself in their shoes, he knew they couldn't help everyone if they wanted to make it back alive. Some might have called her decision callous but he knew that wasn't her. Still, it didn't help when they heard the distant echo of three rounds.

It was a new world with new rules and not everyone would survive.

Chapter 2

The world had gone to hell and he kind of liked it.

Deputy Sam Daniels stood on the back porch of his home in Castine, Maine, smoking a cigarette and listening to the dinging of a buoy bell as it bobbed in the water. A bright sun pushed back the gray morning with a deep orange. Spread before him was Penobscot Bay, its frigid dark waters filled with boats as fishing became the number one source of food.

He glanced at his watch. Except for the few times he needed to go into the department, his cruiser was his mobile office. At any given time he could be patrolling one of ten communities spread out over 2,345 square miles. By now his shift would be in full swing with the Hancock County Sheriff's Office but all that had changed in the blink of an eye.

At first, they figured it was just another outage, some even laughed that someone had screwed up and hit the wrong switch, but when vehicles stopped working, and communication ended, things became drastic.

Mobs took to the streets.

Looting became rampant.

Starvation killed several, and the rest struggled to hold it together.

Now had it occurred in the middle of the summer, they could have continued providing service using bicycles, but with so much snow on the ground, they were left to patrol by foot and the few deputies that showed up for work soon tired of that. Within a month the Ellsworth department was reduced to a skeleton crew.

Born and raised in Castine, he'd told Sheriff Wilson that Carl Madden and him would oversee the small town if only to give the residents a sense that someone was still trying to help. Of course it was a ridiculous task but what else was he supposed to do with his time? Sitting around watching boats might have been good once he retired but he still had a fire in his belly and this provided an opportunity to perform the kind of police work he signed up for, not the one that was hamstrung by a tainted justice system.

While Hancock suffered from its fair share of crime, most of his time had been spent dealing with domestics and the odd theft. But since the blackout, crime had reached new levels. He knew people could be violent but this was another kettle of fish. At this stage he wasn't concerned so much about looting as he was about protecting people's lives. Four months since the blackout, there wasn't anything left to loot except homes.

Over the past few months, Sam had attended numerous town hall meetings that erupted into arguments. He'd seen people point fingers and accuse them of not doing enough but what did they expect? Manpower had been reduced to a handful across the county. They weren't being paid. The department had no transportation and besides a few walkie-talkies there was no communication. Before, if someone was robbed in the middle of the night, a cop could be out there within ten minutes and they could block off roads and often find the culprit before they left the county, but now it was less about stopping crime than it was ensuring that whoever was involved was identified and taken off the streets.

The two of them had tried to do that themselves but had found that it was too overwhelming. He'd been in talks with the town manager and suggested deputizing a few of the locals, people that had demonstrated they could be trusted. It was a tough call. That was where he was meant to be that morning. But first things first — he needed a cup of coffee, a quick shot of caffeine to kick start his day. Then he might feel ready to deal with the crap that was piling up. Forget paperwork, that was a thing of the past. The biggest challenge was determining who was at fault for crime.

With the locals' nerves on edge, many had turned to carrying handguns and weren't afraid to use them, resulting in the death of several people. *They were trespassing. I thought they were going to attack me.* Under normal circumstances, evidence would be compiled, statements taken, lawyers would argue it out in court and a verdict would be reached. But now all they could go on was their word.

That had been the case with Sara Gray.

One of the first people in Castine to kill after the event.

One of the first to come under scrutiny for her actions.

Three dead; one beaten to death and two stabbed. It was a bloody mess, and when questioned all she had to say for herself was that she had no idea what they wanted. It was a hard pill to swallow. People didn't attack without reason. At least not those who were sane. Sure, if they'd been drugged up that might have made sense but according to the local coroner, they were drug free. Had it not been for her boy and Jake Parish, or the fact that she was considered by many to be an upstanding citizen, or the fact that more murders and looting followed, she might have found herself in deep waters.

Sam had tried to come up with some solution, some viable plan of action to deal with it but it was pointless. With every passing month it felt like they were taking twenty steps back in trying to keep the community safe. In the first few weeks they'd tried to get some of the locals on board with sharing supplies but that idea fell on deaf ears. No one was willing to give up what they had and yet in turn they then wondered why houses were being raided by desperate people.

He breathed in deeply trying to enjoy this rare moment in his day. He knew he didn't have to do anything; he could have joined everyone else and pointed a finger but where would that have got them? Besides, that wasn't his way. No, he was only good at one thing and that was policing.

Sam strolled back inside and retrieved a small Jetboil stove that he had for camping and used it to boil up some water. He fished out of the cupboard a pack of coffee and dumped a few spoonfuls into the French press. It was the small things he would miss. Coffee. Cigarettes. They were a luxury now.

"Morning, sunshine," a familiar voice bellowed

He turned to find Carl standing in the doorway. He

was clean shaven, with buzz cut ginger hair and a uniform that had lots of creases.

Great. His timing was impeccable.

"Perfect timing," Carl said. "I'll have a cup too. Hold the cream and sugar."

"Well that's good because I ran out of sugar and cream a month ago." He chuckled and took a seat in his rocking chair out on the porch. "How's the barricade coming along?"

They'd set up two barricades on State Highways 166 and 199, the two main arteries that ran into Castine. It was one of many ideas that were set into motion within the first three weeks of the outage, as looting was rampant and they wanted to catch anyone trying to leave with large amounts of food, and prevent those from outside of the area who had no business in town. It had worked for a while with the assistance of locals but motivation to help soon waned and the group of twenty-five that had been all full of beans to work together soon fell apart. At the last count, they had only six people.

"Don't you mean those who are supposed to be manning it?" Carl replied, pulling out a cigarette and lighting it. He blew gray smoke out of his mouth and squinted as it went up into his eye.

"They're not there?" Sam asked, pausing as he lit the flame to boil the water.

"No, word has it a number of people have left town on foot heading for Bangor. Can you believe that? What a total bunch of idiots."

Sam shrugged. "I don't know, that's where they say that FEMA camps are."

"Oh really?"

"You didn't hear about that?"

"No, I was unable to squeeze that radio time in with patrol and all," he said with a glint in his eye. Word had spread that America was under martial law and the government had set up refugee camps around large cities. They said it was meant to help but he had to wonder. They had yet to see the military roll into their neck of the woods and he didn't expect it either. If their luck of holding on to employees was anything like the local misfortune, the US government was probably running on a skeleton crew as well.

"So who's manning the posts?"

Carl crossed one leg over the other. "No one." He said it like it didn't matter, or he didn't give a shit. "In fact I was thinking we should probably take the damn things down. I mean it's not like there's any food to protect anymore. The stores are empty. Besides what people have in their home, and what folks are bringing in by fishing, I can't see anyone targeting this town. It's too small, too insignificant."

He was right on it being small but insignificant? No. It was because it was small that it would become a target. Larger towns would have more to protect, and no doubt had formed factions that would stand against crime. But here, the lawless could run amok and there wasn't much people could do about it.

"No, let's keep them up."

Carl threw up his hands. "Why?"

"Because of the recent string of murders."

"C'mon, Sam, that was par for the course and you know it,"

"It doesn't mean we should settle for it. The way I see it, Carl, we are the last line of defense against whoever and whatever chooses to target this community."

Carl laughed. "Man, you make me laugh. You see, I've been thinking about that. How long has it been since we saw Wilson?"

"A month and a half but he's got his hands tied."

"Oh I bet he has, banging that woman he was having an affair with before the outage."

"Carl."

"It's true. We all know it. Shit, Sam, we are the only ones dumb enough to still be at this. Davenport and Jenkins. Gone. That's right. They're no longer in Ellsworth. And think, who have we helped so far? Huh?"

"Lots of people."

"Name one."

He was at a loss for words. Carl was once again right,

and he hated that.

"See! If we walked away, things would just continue the way they have. No, I say we kick back, take off the uniforms and ride this out on that boat of yours. You always were complaining you never got enough time to use it. Now's the time before they figure out what caused this damn shitfest, and the lights come back on."

"And if they don't?" Sam asked.

"Don't be so pessimistic."

"Pessimistic? Carl, it's been months. Don't you think if they could have done it, they would have by now?"

"Please. We're talking about our government. You've seen how they operate. It takes them years just to approve one thing in this country. They just need some time. And in the meantime, we take the opportunity to get some serious R and R because when the power comes back on, the boss will have us on back-to-back shifts." Carl then glanced into the house and squinted. "What's that?"

He got up and stepped through the open patio doors and crossed the room to a map of Castine. There were red pins all over it, with string tied between them. Carl let out a laugh. "Oh man. You're killing me here, Sam. You're still vying for that detective position, aren't you, even after all of this?"

"Those are the areas where those women went missing."

Several single women in the area had disappeared from their homes. At first, they notched it up to leaving town as there was no sign of a struggle but no bags had been packed, they'd not given their loved ones any indication they were planning on leaving, and based on those who knew them, that was out of character.

"Seriously, give it up. We barely have the resources to deal with minor crimes but this… forget it."

"Would you if Lucy was one of them?"

Lucy was one of Carl's four daughters. Even though he acted as if he didn't give a shit, he really was a family man at heart, and a community minded guy. That's why he'd held out this long wearing the uniform when other officers had walked off the job.

"You know I would be out there looking but we're facing bigger challenges, Sam."

"What if I said I had a lead?"

"What?" He turned, looking curious.

"The body of one of the three women was found in Witherle Woods. A lady out walking her dog came across her corpse buried in a shallow grave."

"So you've got a body. That doesn't exactly tell us anything, does it? Unless of course this dog walker saw something or the girl had something on her?"

"I'm just saying it's a start. It's something we can sink our teeth into and right now it's probably the only thing we can do."

Carl turned away from the map, uninterested. "Right now hunting down some so-called serial killer is not something to sink our teeth into, it's foolish. Come on, Sam, you can't honestly expect us to waste our time trying to track someone down for crimes that we don't even know are connected. For all we know these women might have left town, and the one in the woods, well...

that's just unfortunate."

"And what about the seven-year-old kid? Or aging parents who were relying on one of them to make sure they got their meds?"

Carl sighed. "No, I get it. Under normal circumstances it would be classed as odd but these are not normal circumstances. They are desperate times. Every man for himself kind of days. People do weird shit."

"At least come over with me to retrieve the body. I said I would get it out of there and talk to Leanne this morning about it."

Leanne was the lady who'd found the body.

Carl brought a hand up to his face and groaned as he looked out across the bay at the boats. "Uh. And there was me thinking we could knock back a few beers and do some fishing today."

"Why, you got beers?"

"No I thought you had some."

He laughed.

"Look, the body was found not far from the Manor

Inn. I was thinking of heading over there at some point today and see if we can speak with Sara Gray. Find out if she heard anything."

"The Sara Gray? The one that annihilated those three intruders?"

"That's the one."

Carl looked back at him with a smirk on his face. "Have you thought for a second that maybe she's behind it? I mean slap my ass and call me Sally, but did you see what she did to those three? That was some crazy shit. I wouldn't put it past her."

Sam smirked. "Why would she do that?"

"I don't know, maybe they didn't pay their bill before leaving the inn."

Sam rolled his eyes and poured out the coffee. "Oh my God," he said. "They were locals, you idiot. Ugh. This is gonna be a long day."

Chapter 3

The lightning bolt struck the ground with such force she felt the earth tremble.

Her father's words came back to her as clear as day. Whatever you do, don't get caught out in an exposed area like a field, a road or on a bald summit. It couldn't have come at a worse time. They'd been on the open road when storm clouds rolled in followed by a low rumble. Had the power grid been up she could have used the AT weather website to get a forecast but now all she had was her senses.

As lightning webbed across the gunmetal sky, she hollered back to Landon to speed it up as they needed to find shelter fast. Beth began counting the seconds to see how long it took until she heard the thunder, as that gave her an indication of how far away it was. Five seconds and they were looking at one mile. She knew you didn't need to be directly under it to be hit by lightning. There had been reports of people being up to twenty-five miles or less away and still being hit. Use the thirty-second rule as a guideline, her father had said.

Drenched by the downfall of rain — seven hours, twenty-two miles later they hurried into a dilapidated church just off Big Dry Run Road to avoid a lightning storm. They could have pitched a tent like most might have while hiking but it was safer to get inside something solid. The glass double doors on the front of the brick building were smashed. It was pitch dark when they stepped in out of the rain. Beth shook the water off like a dog and lifted a small hand-crank flashlight and began cranking on it for a few minutes before a bright light illuminated the dingy guts of the church.

"Oh man, my legs are killing me," Landon said. "Please tell me we aren't going to hike any more tonight?"

"Take a weight off. We've done well for now."

Beth shone the light around, taking in the sight of graffiti, overturned pews and debris scattered all over the floor. There were bottles of beer, a used condom and what looked like a burned pile of Bibles at the center of a red painted pentagram. "What the heck?"

"Okay, that's not creepy at all," Landon said. "Maybe we should brave the storm and keep going."

Another crack of lightning and the sky flashed multiple times.

Beth chuckled. "And get struck by lightning? No thanks, I'll take my chances here." She ambled in, stepping over the mess. It smelled like urine and shit. Someone had really gone to town on the place.

"Satanists," Landon said, pointing to the pentagram. "You'd think they'd have better things to do with their time than desecrate the house of the Lord."

"You religious?" Beth asked washing the light over the walls and trying to read some of the graffiti.

"Me? No. But I have respect for what people believe. I figure if it helps, makes people feel good about life, why not?"

She frowned. "My mother was a big believer."

"Oh yeah?"

"Didn't do her much good though," she said without looking his way. He didn't respond. Landon gave her a hand bringing one of the pews upright so they could have something to bed down on for the night. Beth tossed her pack down and unraveled a sleeping bag on one end while he did the same. "You hungry?"

He shook his head no. They'd stopped a couple of times to eat along the way, and she'd made sure they had enough. Mostly it was jerky and nuts, both were a good source of protein and fat which tended to provide more energy than carbs.

Landon removed his jacket and shook it off before removing a layer of clothing and wiping a bandanna across his rain-soaked face. "Back at the cabin you mentioned your mom. And the cocaine. What happened?"

Beth glanced at him, clenched her jaw but didn't give him the answer he wanted. "I'll check out back, just to make sure things are clear." She shone the light at the floor, and Landon cranked his light on. A glow lit up the inside of the church as she wandered through a set of doors into a dark corridor. She took out her SIG Sauer P320 and scanned the many rooms on either side. One was a nursery, another a room for teenagers, then there were some washrooms and then two offices. Cracking open the door into an office she was pleased to see no one was lying dead inside. They'd encountered a few corpses along the way, those who'd been savagely attacked.

Curious, Beth rooted through drawers and a cupboard.

It was just full of religious books, photographs of a family and some posters of events coming up in the small community. Stepping out of the office she stared at the fire exit which was ajar. Moving on down towards it, she lifted the gun. Someone had jammed a large boulder between the door and frame to hold it open. She shone the light down near her feet and then saw a trail of blood.

Not wanting to find out where it led, she pushed the boulder out of the way and closed the door. Satisfied no one was out back, she exited the rear of the church, her mind distracted by the loud claps of thunder. She hated it. Always had. As she came out, she shone the light over to where Landon was and was just about to ask him something when she noticed he was gone. "Landon?" No answer.

Her gun hand went up and she dropped into a crouch. She slid up along the far wall before stopping and letting her eyes adjust to the darkness. Her heart pounded. "Landon?" Again nothing. Shit. She slid along the wall, one eye on the entrance, the other looking down to make sure she didn't lose her footing.

Right then a figure stepped into view, and she shone the light over.

Landon put up his hands to block the glare. "You mind?"

"Damn it! Where did you go?"

"To take a shit. Is that okay? I wasn't exactly going to go in here, even though it smells like someone already has. You know the saying, don't shit where you sleep."

She brought a hand up to her face and smiled.

"You okay?" he asked.

She nodded and lowered her weapon.

"Anything out back?"

"Not unless you enjoy heavy religious texts."

He chuckled and took a seat on the pew.

She continued. "I'm thinking we should probably block off the doors tonight."

"Why, you having second thoughts about this place?"

"There was blood out back."

"Nosebleed?" Landon asked.

"Would be one hell of a nosebleed."

"Right," he muttered. "Look, I don't think my legs can walk another foot let alone a mile. My Achilles tendon is tight. I have shooting pain going to my knee and I've got a gimpy right leg." He reached into his bag and pulled out some ibuprofen, and gulped it with some of the water from his bag. He then sat down and put his feet on top of his backpack to elevate them and avoid swelling. "Damn things are throbbing."

"You sure you're using the hiking sticks correctly?"

He laughed. "You must think I'm real dumb. Wrap

your hands around the pole and dig it in the earth. The end," he said groaning.

"Not exactly," she replied. "Show me."

He waved her off. "Beth. Go to sleep. I'm fine."

"And yet you're in pain."

"Because I've been hiking for hours. They hurt."

"And they will if you don't use the trekking poles correctly." She knew she probably came across as a know-it-all but there were a lot of folks who never got the full benefit of hiking poles because they figured it didn't require a technique. However everything on the trail had a technique. Hanging food in a tree, purifying water, installing a tent, preventing bug bites and so on.

Landon groaned as he scooped the poles up. He clasped them and showed her. "Happy?"

He was just about to throw them down when she replied, "Well that explains a lot."

"What?"

She shone the light on them. "First off you have the right one in the left hand, and the left in the right."

"They're the same."

"The poles are but not the straps," she said pointing to them. "That's why they mark the poles L and R. The padding on the inside goes further up depending on which pole you are holding." She grabbed his hand. "See that blister. Yeah. Could have been avoided."

"All right, smart-ass."

"Now hold them again."

He did it and she shook her head, touching the back of his arm and raising it.

"What now?"

"You've got to get your arms at a 90-degree angle." She demonstrated. "Now you set the pole based on that angle so that it's comfortable." She took the pole, unscrewed and extended it further then tightened it. "There, try that."

He did it and pursed his lips. "Feels better, I guess." He went to throw them down and she stopped him. He grimaced. "C'mon. There can't be more."

"You're not even using the straps."

"I didn't need them."

"They're there for your benefit," she said. "The strap is to distribute the weight from your lower body to the pole itself."

He slipped his hand into the strap and clasped the pole. "There. Happy?"

She raised her eyebrow and he sighed. "You've got to be joking."

"Hey, it's your body."

"But you're not using any," Landon said.

She shrugged. "How often did you hike before this, Landon?"

"Just show me," he said wanting to avoid embarrassment.

"Okay, well look at your hands. You've gone through the top and look… your hands are in this death grip. That's going to do you no good. A lot of people hold it like that. I want you to go through the bottom of the strap."

"Oh you're just being picky now. Bottom, top, does it

really matter?"

"Try tomorrow and you tell me," she replied. "Through the bottom, up and over and grip the pole. Now you see how the inner padding is covering your hand? If you were holding the other pole, there would be no padding. See what I mean?" she said showing him. He nodded. "Okay, let's move on."

"Move on?" Landon asked. "Are you kidding me?"

She laughed. "Landon. The terrain we walk on isn't all flat. We go up, down, pitch sideways. Don't you want to know how to support your body for stability, rhythm and comfort?"

He motioned with the pole. "Go on then," he said in a non-enthusiastic tone.

"First, show me how you were walking."

"You saw how I was walking. If I was doing it wrong, why didn't you say earlier?"

"Because I was too busy scanning for trouble."

He huffed and trudged forward.

"Stop. Stop," she said pulling a face. "That was awful."

She walked over and took the pole and demonstrated. "Make sure you lead with the pole on the opposite side of the foot you're walking. So if you lead with the right foot you use the left pole and so on." She then went through the process of showing him until she was convinced he had it.

Landon raised his eyebrows. "Are we done?"

"You'll thank me tomorrow," she said as he laid the poles down and settled in for the night. When he sat down, he pulled off his boot and rubbed the back of his foot. "Oh man, that feels glorious. Though I have some gnarly blisters."

She shone the light over and grimaced at two raw bubbles.

Beth dug into her backpack for the first-aid kit and ambled over holding out a needle and a lighter. Landon flinched. "Uh, what are you doing?"

"Popping those blisters."

"No."

"I can tell you it will feel better to do it now than to

wait until it's in your dirty, sweaty sock."

"But…"

"It's fine, I'll sterilize it." She brought up a lighter and heated up the end of the needle. She could have done it in hot water but this was faster. Once that was done, she went to do it and he put his hand out almost stabbing himself.

"I can do it."

"Fine. Just make sure you get it near the bottom so it drains out."

He looked as if he was about to throw up. Once he was done, she handed him some alcohol swabs to clean the wounds, then calendula, a natural alternative to Neosporin, and finally a simple Band-Aid. She could have gone for herbs to help with healing but there was no need. This would do the trick. There was no point making it any more complex than it needed to be. Immediately after that she took out some KT athletic tape.

"What's that for?"

"To reduce friction and offer support to your foot. You want to prevent them, right?"

Once done she noticed he was staring at her.

"What?" she asked.

He shrugged. "You remind me a lot of Ellie. She was thoughtful like you."

Her chin dipped and she tried to shift the topic. It was uncomfortable discussing that which they couldn't change. She missed her father but there was no point living in the past. He wouldn't have wanted her to do that.

"We should get some sleep. We have another big day tomorrow, and hopefully we'll make it to Damascus if we push on. But first let's get those doors barricaded."

It wasn't easy as what remained of the doors had no glass in them, but they managed to stack up some of the pews against the opening. All she wanted was something in place to alert her if anyone tried to get in.

After that he said goodnight and put his head down, using some clothes as a pillow.

She nodded and reached for her bag to suck water out of a tube that went into her backpack. She removed her boots and slipped into the sleeping bag, keeping a firm grip on her handgun. Her mind drifted and it wasn't long before the lightning eased and she heard Landon snoring up a storm. Her eyes roamed the rafters of the building. Large wooden beams crisscrossed over. Outside the wind howled and the rain continued to beat against the earth, its natural rhythm lulling her into sleep. Her eyes grew heavy and just as they were about to close, she heard something, a scuffle nearby.

A shot of fear went through her and Beth scanned the room.

Figures darted across the room. How did they get in?

Then it dawned on her. Maybe they were here all along. But where?

As she was about to pull out her gun, a hand clamped over her mouth.

Chapter 4

Landon gawked at the woman holding a knife to his throat. "We don't want any trouble." His eyes adjusted to the darkness as he scanned the room. His head was pressed down hard against the pew and someone was sitting on his feet. "Beth?"

"I'm here," she replied.

"Get him up," another female said. All he could make out was the silhouette of figures looming over him. The lower half of their faces were masked and they were all wearing hoods. Dragged to his feet, he felt a sharp jab in his kidneys from behind. He groaned and another woman reprimanded the one who'd struck him. "Maya."

"Ruby, I say we hang him now."

"What do you want?" Beth asked. "And who the hell are you?"

Slowly Landon's eyes adjusted and he was able to tell they were surrounded by five figures, all of them were female at least if their voices were anything to go by.

"Shut the hell up, and maybe you'll live. I want a word with him." A female pushed back her hood to reveal short spiky hair. A light off to his right flashed on and he squinted. "What are you doing with her?"

"We're making our way back to Maine," Landon said.

"A likely story. You her father?"

"No."

"So what's a grown-ass man doing with a teenager?"

"He's a friend of mine."

"I said shut up!" The girl spun around and jabbed a knife towards Beth. Beth was being held by two of them. They had her arms and one of them was yanking on her hair.

"Look, what's your name?" Landon asked.

"Why, you want to try to lure me into your sick world?"

"I don't know what you…"

Before he could get the words out, she slapped him across the face with the back of her hand. "You keep opening that dirty mouth of yours and maybe I will let Willow here hang you from these rafters. Now I want some honest answers. This is of course the house of the Lord, that is what you said, right?"

She'd heard him. Ruby looked up. "You should look up more often."

That's where they'd been hiding in the darkest corners of the building, high up in the rafters. "So let me ask you again. Why are you traipsing through our neck of the woods with a young girl?"

"I just told you. We're going home to Maine."

"You from Maine?"

He frowned. "I just said that."

"Not you. I'm asking her," she said without taking her eyes off Landon.

Beth replied. "No. North Carolina. But…"

Someone punched her in the gut preventing her from speaking any further.

"North Carolina and Maine. Want to fill in the gaps?" she asked.

Landon spoke up. "I crashed. I mean, the plane I was in landed in the mountains near her cabin. She helped me."

"Helped you? That's not a good idea." She sucked air between her lips and shook her head as she paced in front of him, staring him up and down. "You see, around here men like you only want one thing." She sniffed hard and scowled at him. "No, I'm not buying the plane crash. You see, the other day we came across two guys with a female. Do you think she told the truth?" She waited for a reply but Landon didn't answer. "They had brainwashed her. How do I know? Dixie!" she said. A sixth girl emerged from the shadows, young, no older than fourteen. "Meet Dixie. The girl we rescued, isn't that right, Dixie?" She nodded. "Those men were animals. They killed her family and then took her with them for their own pleasure. Animals. Just like you."

"You've got this wrong. I had a daughter."

"Yeah? Where is she?"

"Dead. She died in the plane crash."

"Oh, so you're taking this one to fill the hole, are you?" There was silence before she continued. "Well?" she asked in a slow manner.

"If you would just let me speak," Beth said.

Ruby turned in a flash and charged over to her, grabbed her by the neck and looked as if she was about to tear into her but instead, she planted a kiss on her lips and ran a hand over Beth's breasts. Beth managed to pull her face away. "Stubborn. I like that. Lilith will like that."

"Lilith your mother?" Landon asked.

Ruby turned and squinted at him. "Lilith. Oh she'll enjoy you too. Though I haven't decided yet whether or not I'll take you back. I might just kill you here. So how about you tell me the truth before I have Willow hang you and do what we did to those two men. What did we do, Willow?"

Willow laughed. "Cut their balls off and hung 'em till they bled out."

"Pleasant," Landon said. "Four months and you're doing that? And you think men are animals."

She didn't like that. Ruby rushed forward and grabbed him by the throat.

"Gonna kiss me as well?" he said. That was the worst thing he could have said. She took the knife in her hand and pressed it up against his face then slid it down. Landon let out a cry as it sliced into his cheek.

"Tell me the truth."

"Fuck you!" Landon said, spitting in her face.

The girl raised the blade as Beth cried out. "Stop. You're right. He took me."

"Beth?" Landon said. "What the…?"

Ruby turned her head, casting a glance over her shoulder.

"He killed my father, shot my mother and then took me. We were on a run for food. He told me not to say anything otherwise his pals would kill my sister."

What the hell was she playing at? Obviously, she was lying. Was this just a trick? If it was, what was her end game? How the hell were they meant to get out of this? Landon studied her face but it was just expressionless.

"I knew it," Ruby replied. "We've yet to meet one man along this road who isn't a dirty sicko." She walked over to Beth "And what's your name, darlin'?"

"Beth Sullivan."

She smiled then looked back. "Hang him up, Willow. Give this animal what he deserves!"

"No," Beth said, cutting in as Willow threw a noose over Landon's neck and tightened it. "I mean, if you do that my sister is as good as dead."

"Sister?"

"They've got her."

"How many are there?" Ruby asked.

"Seven," Beth shot back without hesitation.

"Where?"

"A few miles south of here holed up on a farm. I can take you to them. Maybe you can help get my sister back. Look, I'm sorry I didn't come clean but..." Beth looked over at Landon. "I've..."

"No need to explain. We get it. Us girls have to stick together. Right?"

Beth nodded and gave a strained smile.

Ruby tapped the air with her finger and looked over at Landon. "Though I still think he deserves to die."

"He does," Beth added quickly. "But we'll need him at least for a while. They're a nervous group. If he doesn't show his face, they will kill her in an instant."

Good. Good work, Beth. I just hope you've figured this out, he thought.

Ruby paced in front of him, spinning her knife like a drumstick, then slapping it against her hand.

"She's right. We should let Lilith decide," Maya said.

Ruby nodded. "Fine. Let's take him back."

"Beth. Beth!" he yelled as they dragged him out into the rain. "Don't do this, they'll kill her!" He played into whatever she was up to. With a noose still over his neck, one of them tied his wrists together, dragged him to an old Jeep and tossed him in the back. Three of the women jumped in and sat on the edge looking down at him with disgust. One had a Beretta inches away from his face. Under the flash of lightning he could see them better.

Each of them wore dark figure-hugging clothing and heavy military-style boots. They couldn't have been more than twenty-five.

The Jeep's engine roared to life and he went to get up after hearing Grizzly bark. He wanted to see if Beth was coming with them but was quickly forced down by multiple feet. "Stay put, you piece of shit," a girl said before spitting in his face. The Jeep tore out of the church's parking lot and peeled away into the night.

Throughout the short journey, Landon was regretting playing along with Beth.

What if this backfired on them? Dying at the hands of a group of misandrists was not how he wanted to go out. He always envisioned himself going in his sleep, or quickly as a plane's nose bombed into the ocean, not having his nuts cut off and fed to him.

It didn't take long to arrive. When the Jeep came to a stop, he was hauled out and pushed forward towards a one-story wooden building at the edge of a road. To gain his bearings he scanned the road before entering and spotted a sign that read Roan Creek Road. His eyes lifted to a neon sign that wasn't lit up but had the words: Neva Grill. Thrust inside a sweating room full of women, he recognized the place as a greasy spoon diner. There was a long bar with small silver stools, behind it whitewashed walls. The floor was a checkered black and white and the booths that went around the edges were an aqua green leather.

Dance music was playing from a speaker in the corner of the room. It had to have been powered by solar as since the blackout he hadn't heard any music. Scantily clad women in cut-off jean shorts, and black and red bras, paraded down the bar dancing and jiggling their asses in the faces of other women who sat there tossing green notes at them like it was a strip joint. It reminded him of the movie *Coyote Ugly* except these women were butt ugly. He had to wonder if they'd been crossbred with cows as all that shit they were shaking around looked worse than a pair of cracked udders.

Heads turned as he was thrust down the aisle between

the booths to his right and diner counter to the left. Women of all ages spun on stools, one shot out her leg and he tripped over it landing face first on the floor. They roared with laughter. What the hell was this place? As he was dragged to his feet and pushed on, a woman in her late thirties who was missing a tooth reached out and groped him before planting a kiss on his cheek. One by one they poked, prodded and slapped him.

He felt like a lamb being led to the slaughter. At a rough headcount there had to have been at least twenty, maybe thirty women of all ages.

"You seen Lilith?" Ruby appeared at his side and asked a black woman with thick dreadlocks who was in the middle of running her hand up some girl's leg.

She looked back with an annoyed expression and gave a nod. "In the VIP room."

A hand clasped his jacket and he was shoved toward double doors that led into a kitchen. It had been gutted and turned into a lounge with sofas and a bed at the center. As he entered, and the doors swung closed behind them, Ruby cleared her throat to get the attention of three half naked women sprawled out on the bed. Two of them parted to reveal an attractive white-haired woman. She licked her lower lip and looked him up and down. "Get out of here," she said to the other two. She slapped one woman's naked cheeks and they hurried past them.

The woman swung her legs off the bed, not bothering to cover herself, and she walked up to him. She was slender, tall, around six foot, and in incredible shape. "Take a look. I know you want to," she said getting really close to his face, her mouth widening as if trying to inhale his aroma. It was awkward, he didn't know where to direct his eyes.

"What have we got, Ruby?"

"Found him and a girl inside the church."

"Ah. Repenting of your sins, were you?"

"Oh he admitted his crime," Ruby replied.

Landon swallowed hard and tried to look over his shoulder through an opening in the wall where the cook would usually take orders. *Where are you, Beth?*

"Look, there's been a mistake."

"Oh a mistake was made. When men were born," she said with a hint of venom. There was a clear disdain at the very mention of men. He recalled Max showing him a video online of a woman on the streets of New York going nuts on a group of guys protesting abortion. Her argument had less to do with abortion than with them being men and having any say in what women wanted to do with their bodies. Max thought it was hilarious. Landon had switched it off and told him it was best to spend his time on promoting equality rather than taking a side over matters he knew nothing about. Max had told him that wasn't why he was watching it. He just thought the lady's reaction was insane.

"And the girl? Where is she?" Lilith asked.

"Out front. She says his pals are holding her sister. I wanted to get your go-ahead to take a group and get her back."

"How many?"

"Seven, maybe more."

The woman got close to Landon. "Sure. Take care of business and leave him with me." Ruby gave a nod and backed out of the room like this woman was some kind of goddess. It was the strangest shit he'd ever seen. He tried pinching himself to see if it was some weird dream. He figured he'd awake inside the church and notch it up to some nightmare caused by the pentagram on the church floor.

The woman turned and glanced over her shoulder to watch him as she walked across the room and slipped into some tight jeans, making sure to bend in front of him. Once dressed in shirt and boots, she picked up a packet of smokes and lit one.

She offered him one but he shook his head.

After blowing out smoke she sat in a wicker chair a few feet away.

"You know, I was fourteen when a close friend of my family took advantage of me. I tried telling my father but you know what he said?" She paused for effect. "Lilith, you have a wild imagination. Stop lying."

ALL THAT SURVIVES: A Post-Apocalyptic EMP Survival Thriller

Landon didn't know what to say.

"The man continued until one day I took a razor in my mouth and went down on him. You should have heard him scream. He never touched me again after that," she said. "But that's not the best part. When I told the cops what happened, you know what they did? Handed me over to child services. I bounced around foster home to foster home until I was of an age to leave the system." She sucked on the cigarette, relishing each drag, her eyes rolling back in her head. He had to wonder if there was something else in it as it gave off a strange smell. "That man used to own this restaurant. Now look." She waved her arms around. "Fate has a wicked sense of humor, don't you think?"

Chapter 5

Beth imagined she would die in these gloomy dark woods. She had been certain they would get farther than this in the journey. Not long after dropping off Landon, she was told to wait in the battered old Jeep with three other women. Ruby emerged with another five. The skies had opened up and rain was turning the gravel in front of the restaurant into a stream. Ruby brought up her hood and jogged over to the passenger side. "You tell Willow which way to go, and we'll follow." She squeezed Beth's arm. "We'll get her back."

She had to think fast.

They would be expecting her to take them to a farm full of men.

The thumping of her heart in her ears drowned out the roar of the Jeep as it came to life and Willow veered out, heading back toward the church. Desperately, she tried to calm herself.

You can lie, they won't know any different.

They trust women over men.

ALL THAT SURVIVES: A Post-Apocalyptic EMP Survival Thriller

While it made sense to her, she was beginning to worry. They had taken their bags and removed her bow, machete and SIG Sauer. Even if she could convince them to not kill Landon, there was no way in hell they would let them walk off together. Her stomach churned as the Jeep bounced over potholes full of water and she guided Willow along the dark and narrow road. Pine trees whipped by in her peripheral vision as she scanned the homes along Big Dry Run Road.

"Anything stand out to you?" Willow asked.

She shook her head. "Nothing so far."

Willow hadn't taken her eyes off Beth since the church. Unlike the others, who seemed pleased to have another woman amidst them, Willow looked less impressed. "You know there are a few things that don't add up about you."

"Yeah? Like what?" Beth asked.

"Why didn't you just kill him? You had a gun on you."

"For the same reason I didn't want you to kill him.

These men aren't idiots. If I returned to the farm without him, they would have killed my sister."

"Sister. Right. And this sister of yours. She got a name?"

"Tristan."

"Tristan?"

She repeated the name with a tone of skepticism.

"And how old is she?"

"Nine."

"And they took both of you."

"That's right."

"How long ago?"

The questions just kept coming. She was hitting her from every angle. Trying to find a hole, a flaw, hesitation in her voice, anything that would give her reason to disbelieve her story. Beth assumed not everyone would buy her story, in fact she was surprised they believed her enough to send out women to help.

Wanting to change the topic, Beth asked, "So what's the deal with you all? I mean some of you must have had brothers, fathers. What happened to them?"

Willow chuckled and looked at the two girls in the back.

"Nothing they didn't have coming to them," she said before quickly switching the conversation back to her interrogation. "So why did they give you a gun?"

"Why are you armed?" Beth said throwing it back at her. "These are dangerous times. Can't be too safe."

"No. Can't be too safe." Willow shook her head, narrowing her gaze.

"That way," Beth said pointing to a sign for Mill Creek Road.

"You sure?"

"Positive."

They continued down the slick road, the windshield wipers whipping back and forth. *Quick. You need to pick a farm and fast, otherwise she won't believe you.*

"That one."

"That one?" she asked as if she knew the owner.

"I think," Beth said. "Everything looks the same. I'm

not sure."

"Yeah. It's definitely not that one," Willow added.

Willow didn't explain but she didn't need to. These were local women. They obviously knew who lived in these homes. Why had she told them only two miles? She should have said farther, far outside the boundaries of their small rural community.

They continued on for another five minutes.

The Jeep behind them flashed its lights twice and Willow pulled over to the edge of the road. "What are you doing?" Beth asked nervously.

"Stay here." She shut off the engine and hopped out taking the keys with her but not before flashing Beth a skeptical look. Beth cast a glance over her shoulder and watched her meet Ruby halfway between the two vehicles. A conversation ensued and then Ruby walked back with Willow but came around to the passenger side.

"You having problems remembering?" Ruby asked.

"It's dark. It's been a few days. Every house along here looks the same," Beth said hoping to delay or postpone it until the following morning. "I'm not sure I can find it at night."

Willow was unconvinced. "You said it was two miles south. Why were you sleeping in the church?"

"Willow," Ruby said.

"I'm just asking. Don't you find it a little odd? Both of them had backpacks, and she was armed. Maybe there is some substance to his story."

"No. How many men have we stopped over the last month?"

"A lot."

"And how many were telling the truth?"

"None. But that could be because they were afraid to die."

Ruby narrowed her gaze at Willow.

"I'm just saying. Why would you sleep at a church two miles away from the location you were staying at? Something doesn't add up. I think she's full of shit."

"You can think what you like. You're not the one calling the shots," Ruby replied. She looked back at Beth.

"Willow has a point though. Why did you choose to bed down two miles from the location you came from?"

Beth swallowed hard. Willow smiled as if expecting to be proven right. Then it came to her. "He wanted me for himself. Okay. He didn't want to share with the others. So we were leaving and then we got caught in the lightning storm and well, we took shelter. It was only meant to be for an hour or two and then we were planning on continuing on."

"Bullshit," Willow said. "We heard you approach and saw you enter. You didn't act like he was a threat. Hell, you were the one who went out back. If you wanted to get away from him you had the opportunity."

"I just told you why. He would have gone back and told the others."

"Why didn't you kill him then?"

Beth brought a hand up to her face. "Man, you are dumb."

"What did you say?" She went for Beth but Ruby intervened getting between them. Ruby pulled Willow away and Beth could hear them arguing.

"She's lying."

"If she is, Lilith will handle it."

"Might be too late."

Ruby put a finger up to Willow's face then turned and walked back to Beth. "You've got twenty minutes to find this farm or else." With that said she trudged back to the Jeep behind them and Willow got into the driver's side and glared at her.

"You might have them convinced but not me."

They drove on for another ten minutes. The road forked and they went down Gambell Springs Lane until she just decided on a farm. "That one. That's it."

She held her breath, hoping, praying that Willow didn't know the owners.

"Well let's do this then," she said swerving to the mouth of the driveway that led up to a two-story white house with a large garage and a red barn off to the right of that. All the women hopped out and checked the magazines in their handguns and rifles. Ruby and five other women joined them.

"This is it?" Ruby asked.

Beth nodded. "I can go with you. Just give me my bow."

"Not likely. You're staying here with Willow. Keep an eye on her."

"I intend to," she said, her lip curling up.

Beth watched as the women fanned out and disappeared into the darkness. She knew she had only minutes before they realized that the home was either empty or had different owners. Willow twisted in the driver's seat, her hand resting on the wheel, ready to honk the horn if Beth tried anything. She tapped a handgun against her leg. "I can't wait to see the look on Ruby's face when she returns and I was right."

"You mean, when you were wrong," Beth replied.

Willow chuckled then grabbed Beth's head and slammed it against the dashboard. Beth groaned and reached for her nose which was now gushing blood. With her head down, Willow berated her. "You must think I'm as stupid as them."

Beth could taste iron as blood ran into her mouth. Then an idea came to her. She kept her jaw open and let the blood that was streaming out of her nose fill the lower portion of her mouth.

"But here's the thing." As Willow raised her hand off the horn to wag a finger in Beth's face, she took advantage of the moment and spat the mouthful of blood into her eyes. Willow instinctively brought her hands up to wipe the blood away while cursing but it was too late. Beth reared back her fist and plowed it into her jaw as hard as she could, then followed through with one to the throat. She attempted to twist the gun out of Willow's hand but it went off. *Shit. They would hear that.* She knew she had even less time before they returned. She bent back one of her fingers and broke it to pry the gun loose from her hand while simultaneously jamming her forearm into Willow's neck and holding her back against the seat to prevent her reaching the horn. Back and forth they wrestled in the cramped space for control until Beth forced her out of the vehicle. Both of them landed hard in the dirt with Beth on top of Willow. She pressed her face into the wet soil, looking up every few seconds to make sure the women weren't coming. Nothing. Just pure darkness.

Willow thrashed below her as Beth dug her knee into her back and reached for a knife in a sheath on Willow's leg. As her fingers clawed along Willow's jeans, Willow did a reverse elbow into Beth's gut. It winded her but she refused to let go. Grasping the knife she jammed it into the back of Willow's neck.

A slight gasp escaped her lips, then she stopped resisting. Acting fast, Beth took the knife and hurried over to the Jeep behind her and stabbed two of the tires. Air gushed out deflating them. She sprinted back to the other Jeep, hopped in and fired it up, backing out just as Ruby and the others emerged from the tree line.

Rounds snapped over her head, a couple punctured the Jeep's frame as she tore out.

The last thing she heard was Ruby calling her name.

Chapter 6

They had survived a snowstorm, an attack by three thugs and four months without power. But now Sara was faced with an even greater challenge:

Hungry bellies.

Food wasn't the issue as they had been living off fish from the bay, but cooking was — more specifically coming up with different ways to cook fish. Bake, sauté, fry, boil, grill, poach and steam, she'd tried them all and used every kind of herb available. It really didn't help. She'd grown up loving it but now she would have been glad if she never saw another fish again.

They'd blown through the supplies they had which didn't take long at all with one extra mouth to feed. Since that fateful night when they were attacked, Jake hadn't let her out of his sight. Had she not invited him to stay in one of the fourteen rooms, he would have threatened to pitch a tent out front. In all honesty she was moved that he cared enough to focus his attention on her.

Be grateful, Sara reminded herself. You're alive.

But she wasn't grateful. Landon and Ellie weren't here and she had no idea what had become of them. Sara felt their absence, an overwhelming sadness rested heavy on her chest every day she woke up without them. She didn't want to believe what Hank had said about a small charter plane crashing into the bay but now she was beginning to have her doubts. All she knew was the country had suffered greatly and many had already succumbed to poor sanitation, hunger, cold and violence.

And it wasn't like she could point the finger. Much of that violence came from trying to protect family. How many others across the United States had taken up arms against their own kind to protect their own kin? How many more would die before government would fix this situation?

"You need a hand, dear?" Rita asked. After the death of Hank, Sara couldn't help but feel that she was to blame in some strange way. Sure, she hadn't asked Hank to show up but he had and if he hadn't, perhaps he would still be alive. Still, Rita was getting on in years and until Hank's death he'd handled pretty much everything for her. In fact in the four months she'd been staying at the inn, she'd learned a lot about how manipulative Hank had been. He'd kept his bank accounts separate, only gave Rita a small amount of money each month for spending, and he handled all the bills so she couldn't see all the money that was being spent on escorts. Sara thought Rita would be devastated when she learned of Hank's passing but she wasn't. She simply pursed her lips and nodded. Was there grief? She was sure there was but maybe Rita didn't show it the way others did. Anyway, Sara had invited her to come and stay at the inn. They could pool resources and take care of one another. At first Rita was hesitant but after a few single women started going missing in town she'd taken the offer.

It had worked out well. They now had two gas generators to power the house. They mostly used them to power the electric stove, and the other one for light in the evenings. They were very cautious of how and when they used gas as fuel had become almost non-existent. The little that was to be found was siphoned from vehicles in town or stalled along the main highways into Hancock County. The trouble was everyone had the same idea and over the past month Jake kept returning with even less.

"Oh, if you want to peel the potatoes that would be great," she said.

Rita Thomas was in her early sixties. A full-breasted woman with short wiry hair, she always had a glow to her skin. Dressed in a thick cream cardigan and black slacks she ambled over and took over peeling. Sara assumed she'd be moping around the inn after Hank's death and wanting to talk about it every day, but she hadn't. She immediately started contributing and busying herself in the greenhouse which Jake had constructed to grow and store vegetables.

"Tess still coming for dinner?" Rita asked.

"Yes, she's bringing Ian. Hopefully I can convince him to move into the inn."

So much had changed in Castine, it had become a brittle shell of its former self. Unlike some towns that would band together to help one another, many in town had either headed for the FEMA camp reported to be in Bangor or they kept to themselves. She couldn't blame them; trust was at an all-time low. They'd already seen several murders, one of which included Meg, the owner of the local grocery store. No one knew who was behind it only that they'd shot her and stolen what few supplies she had left for herself.

That's why Sara had set about trying to change that.

With the sheer number of rooms in the inn it seemed a waste to not have some of her closest friends and neighbors under one roof, working together. Janice and Arlo Sterling were still considering it, which was code for "Arlo is being an ass."

But he wasn't the only one. Not everyone was eager or saw the benefits.

Her best friend Tess Hudson would have moved in on the first day of the event but her husband, Ian, thought it would only end in disaster. The truth was he wasn't much of a social bee. Prior to the outage he'd run his own successful construction business and so he tended to spend most of his time working, all of which left Tess to get into trouble. She'd already had two affairs that Ian had no idea about. *It's just a little fun,* she'd said. *You should try it. What they don't know doesn't hurt them. Besides, am I meant to settle for ten seconds of humping like jackrabbits at the end of the night before he rolls over and falls asleep? What about my needs?* Tess cracked her up. She was such a loon.

She cast a glance at Jake who was mending one of the doors that had been torn off its hinges when the three thugs had attacked. She would have been lying to say she wasn't attracted to him. Having him around had only unseated strong feelings that had been there since they were kids. There was something about the way the conversation flowed. They'd often spend time at the end of the day playing cards, or having a glass of wine. Max had begun to take notice and had called her out on it. But she'd been quick to make it clear that they were just friends. She wouldn't do that to Landon. She couldn't. Sara stared out the window wondering where he was or if he was even alive.

"Yoo-hoo!" a familiar voice called out after a brief knock. Sara glanced down the hall to see Tess entering with a small box in hand. Ian walked in with a scowl on his face. Tess had fiery red hair, a flamboyant set of curls that extended past her shoulders. An overly tall woman, she looked a little gangly in certain clothes but most guys didn't notice, they were too focused on the goods, as Tess put it. The very mention of having kids turned her off. She said it was because she didn't have the time to raise a child but Sara knew she valued her body more.

Ian on the other hand was a short ass. He had to tilt his head to look up at her. A stocky man with a buzz cut, he looked as if he was stitched into the shirts he wore.

Sara made a gesture. "Jake, you think you can…"

He looked up and smiled. "Don't worry about it. I'll speak with him."

They'd already discussed how valuable it could be to have Ian at the house. While Jake was handy, having another man around the house to pitch in would not only take some of the load off Jake when he went out to fish but it would give them a greater sense of security. She was hoping Jake could help him see the upside. There really was an upside. Sure, more people meant more mouths to feed but it was no different than if they were living alone. At least together they could lean on one another for support. They could take turns fishing, keeping an eye on the grounds, and enjoy one another's company. With no TV or internet, life in the first month or two had been tough. She didn't realize how addicted or rather, reliant on technology she had become. Now they were back to creating their own entertainment, and entertainment was needed. In a world without power, even if there was a generator, each day was hard.

"Hey, gorgeous. Look what I've brought," Tess said pulling a large bottle of red wine out of the box. She glanced over at Jake and smiled. "Jake."

"Tess," he replied before greeting Ian and leading him away for a beer.

Tess turned back to Sara and flashed her eyes. She'd been lapping it up ever since Sara had told her that Jake had moved in. She wanted details. All the nitty gritty on whether or not they were sharing a bed and what other things was he fixing around the house. The sexual innuendos never stopped with her.

"Any luck?" Sara asked.

"Don't even go there. He's a stubborn mule." Tess looked over at Rita. "Hi Rita."

Rita gave a nod. Sara was hoping Janice would move in if only for the sake of Rita. They were good friends and around the same age so it would offer her some company.

"Come on, pour us a glass and let's go have a natter before dinner. You don't mind handling the food, do you, Rita?" she said, wrapping a hand around Sara's arm and dragging her away. Sara mouthed the word sorry to Rita before disappearing out of the room.

"Tess, I was in the middle of cooking."

"Ah leave it to Rita, it will give her something to do and we can talk about Mr. Luscious."

"I really wish you would stop calling him that."

"Why? He is. I'm surprised it's taken you this long to make a move."

"I've not made a move."

"You invited him to move in. I'd say that's a move."

They walked into the sunroom, a long conservatory that offered a beautiful view in the day. "He wanted to keep a close eye on me."

"I bet he did. Naughty boy," she said in a cheeky way as she opened the wine and poured her a glass. "Here, get that down you." They took a seat on a brown leather sofa and Tess kicked off her shoes and curled up. "Anyway, I hope he can get Ian to see the light. It will be like our old college days living under the same roof. Who knows, maybe we can…"

"Don't even say it," Sara said, cutting her off. She'd become quite adept at knowing when Tess was going to drop into her dirty mind pool and pull out something that would make her cringe. Tess laughed then got all serious.

"So you haven't heard anything from Landon or Ellie?"

She bit down on her lower lip before taking a large gulp of wine. "Nothing."

Tess placed a hand on hers. "They'll be fine, hon. I'm sure they're just caught up in Alabama. You'll see." That was the thing about Tess. One minute she could act like a real loon, and the next show empathy. Maybe that's why they'd been friends so long.

Sara downed her drink and poured another.

"Whoa, slow down," Tess said. "Remember, I'm the one who usually drinks you under the table."

Sara lowered her chin and gave a pained expression.

Tess frowned. "What is it?"

"Nothing."

"Sara. I've known you long enough to know you're a bad liar. C'mon, what's on your mind?"

"What isn't?" Her eyes began welling up.

Tess put her drink down and got up and put an arm around her. "It's your mom, isn't it?"

"No. It's…" She blew out her cheeks and slumped down, taking another swig of her wine. "I've not been sleeping very well since that night. I can't seem to get them out of my head."

"Look, you did what you had to! For Max. For yourself. I would have done the same." She rolled her eyes. "Okay, I admit I probably would have been killed but if those bastards had walked into my house and I managed to kill them, I wouldn't be losing sleep over it. It's not your fault. Don't go beating yourself up. Okay? It's in the past."

"That's the thing, it doesn't feel like it. I keep seeing them. I've tried using alcohol and melatonin to get some sleep but I wake up in a cold sweat, screaming, and then I have to go into Max's room just to make sure he's safe." More tears welled up. "I just wish this was over. That Landon was here and…"

Tess gripped her hand. "I'm here. I'm not going

anywhere. Nor is Mr. Luscious."

Sara snorted through her tears.

Right then Rita came into the room. "Sara, Deputy Daniels is here to see you."

Sara glanced at Tess, a frown forming, and Tess shrugged. She made her way out to the kitchen to find him and Deputy Madden. Carl was an old friend of the family, someone she went to school with, and Daniels was a local who kept to himself. Her heart stopped, thinking he was bringing news about Landon and Ellie. "Is there a problem?"

"No problem. I was just hoping to speak to you about the missing women."

Chapter 7

The Jeep fishtailed around a corner. Beth almost lost control of the Jeep as she pressed the accelerator to the floor. She scanned her mirrors looking for any sign of the women. Even though she knew they couldn't follow in a vehicle with two deflated tires, her fears got the better of her. "Damn it. Damn it!" she yelled, smashing her fist against the steering wheel. There was no time for celebrating her escape. Now she had to figure out how to get Landon out of a restaurant packed with women.

Shit! Shit! She suddenly realized. What if the other Jeep had a two-way radio? Ruby could alert the others and then Landon would be as good as dead and she'd find herself being hunted by an army of psychos.

Her knuckles were white by the time she saw the restaurant. Instead of pulling up outside, she veered off to the edge of the road and drove the vehicle into the woodland. She shut off the lights and went around to the back of the Jeep to collect her bow, handgun and rifle. Their backpacks were still there. If she could get Landon out, they could put some serious miles between them and here but that relied on making sure those crazy bitches couldn't follow. She geared up by slinging her rifle strap over her shoulder, slipping her bowie knife back into the sheath on her hip and checking the magazine in her handgun before taking off on foot.

Hurrying through a barren woodland that was still trying to give birth to leaves, she saw the restaurant come into view. She surveyed the lot out front for movement, watching for anything at all. Her jaw was clenched as she tried to stay in control of her emotions.

She unsnapped the holster in preparation and moved in on the lot.

Puncture the tires on the vehicles out front, get Landon and get the hell out of there, she told herself. It was ominously quiet. The music was no longer playing as she slid up beside one vehicle and dug her knife into a tire. It hissed, air ejecting fast. Trees all around were motionless, the branches still, and no birds were chirping as if a predator was nearby. Other than the rain beating against the ground, the only sounds Beth could hear were her own: the rustle of her legs, the hiss of another tire, and the rhythm of her breathing.

The air was cold and crisp, and in the darkness a wisp of white appeared in front of her mouth. Once the vehicles' tires were slashed, she circled around the restaurant looking for a side door, one that would have been used by staff to throw out trash.

There it was. Steel. Near an industrial dumpster.

Jogging at a crouch she approached and gave the handle a tug.

It cracked open, letting out a slight groan. The light from inside cut into the darkness. A generator could be heard churning away.

The music was still playing but very lightly. She could hear women laughing, and the clinking of glasses. Everyone was enjoying themselves. Ruby hadn't alerted them.

"Come on, Lilith, let me have a little fun with him."

Beth stepped inside and worked her way along the wide corridor littered with boxes of food. She stopped for a second and looked into one, noticing they were full. Were they sending out women into homes around the area to collect food? Had they killed all the men in town? It seemed too outrageous to be true. Then again, she'd met her fair share of women that took things to the edge before the outage. Keeping her fingers on the bow and arrow, she moved stealthily towards the sounds of voices coming from the kitchen.

She could have used the handgun but the last thing she needed was having a gun erupt and alerting all those women at the front of the restaurant.

"Just go away and keep an eye out for Ruby. I want to talk with him — alone!"

As Beth made it to the double doors that led into the kitchen, she peered through a panel of glass. Landon was seated, his body bound to a chair with rope. A tall, attractive woman with sheer white hair stood across from him lighting a cigarette. She tipped her head and blew smoke in the air.

"Castine, Maine. Tell me more?" She said.

Beth stole a glance over her shoulder to make sure no one was coming up behind her before she used the tip of her boot to open the door ever so slowly. The slightest groan and the woman might alert the others. She just needed to get it wide enough to bring up the bow.

"What do you want to know?" Landon replied.

As she pushed through the doorway, Beth raised the bow aiming at the woman's back. Landon saw her before the woman did. His gaze shifted and with it the woman turned her head.

"Don't move, don't breathe or I will end you where you stand," Beth said in a low voice, her eyes scanning the door across the room and a window on the far side where she could just make out women in the room next door. "Now cut him loose."

"You must be the young girl found with him. Where's Ruby?"

"Are you hard of hearing?" Beth replied then swallowed. "Cut him loose."

The woman's lip curled. "You're making a mistake. We can help you here. Out there, you're just bait for people like him."

"I won't tell you again," Beth added, pulling back on the bowstring. The woman nodded slowly and reached for a knife. "And you make any sudden movement, or touch him with that knife and you'll be pulling an arrow out of your neck."

"You know, I like your courage. We could use someone like you," she said dropping down in front of Landon and slicing his restraints. The rope dropped to the floor and he got up and moved past the woman. Beth was very aware that she could have stabbed Landon but something was preventing her from doing so. What? Landon took Beth's handgun and they began backing out the way she came in.

"How far do you think you will get?"

Beth didn't reply but kept moving.

"You'll be back."

"The fuck I will!" she said.

The woman smiled. "Thirty seconds. That's how long I'll give you then it's a free for all." As soon as they were out of view, both of them bolted towards the side door and out into the night.

"Are you out of your mind?" Landon said. "Which way?" Without saying a word she ran and he followed limping ever so slightly. They came around the restaurant and she kept her eyes on the windows as they hurried down the road towards the Jeep. "We'll never make it," Landon said.

After veering off the main road, down an embankment and into the tree line, Beth went over to the driver's side. "Get in."

"Where did you get this?"

"Get in," she said not wanting to waste time explaining.

Landon glanced in the back and saw the bags. "You just keep surprising me," he said. Beth fired up the Jeep and smashed her foot against the accelerator to reverse out. The Jeep whipped out of the tree line and back onto the road. Headlights lit up the road ahead and with it a large group of women coming out of the restaurant. She floored it and the Jeep zipped up Roan Creek Road coming under heavy fire of assault rifles. Rounds punctured the vehicle in multiple places as they tore past the restaurant and Beth caught sight of the woman again. She looked back in her rearview mirror at the rabble rushing to the center of the road, some trying to pursue on foot while others hopped into vehicles only to realize they had flats.

All the while Landon looked over his shoulder.

"How the hell did you pull that off?"

"Does it matter?"

"I thought you had thrown me under the bus."

"To hang out with those lunatics? Please, give me some credit," she said focusing on the road. Landon was breathing hard and trying to catch his breath. He reached over his shoulder and pulled his bag up front. "The bags."

"They were already in the vehicle," she said.

"Come on, Beth, how did you pull it off? The last I heard you were heading with Ruby to some farm."

She sighed and brought him up to speed. As soon as she was finished, he went silent and nodded. "You had to do what you had to do, right?"

"It was either that or die out there."

It didn't take long before the headlights washed over a sign for Mountain City. It was less than ten minutes from the restaurant. "Maybe we should go around."

"That will add at least another hour onto our time," she said squinting at the gas gauge. "And I don't think we have enough fuel to cover that."

"Well we won't be able to drive this all the way to Maine."

"I wasn't planning on that but if we can make it to Damascus, we can at least put some distance between us and them."

"Lilith you mean," he said.

"That's her name?"

"Yeah, batshit crazy woman."

"Anyway the sooner we can get off the main road and join the Appalachian Trail, the better. We'll dump this in Damascus." She snorted tapping the fuel gauge. "That's if we make it there."

"Kill the headlights," Landon said.

She shut them off and the road went extremely dark. The only light came from a crescent moon, and a sky full of stars.

As they got closer to Mountain City, she eased off the gas, seeing the road was blocked. "Ah man, looks like we might be losing this sooner than I thought." She veered to the edge of the road and they stared at the vehicles that had been pushed into place blocking off entry. US-421 cut straight through Mountain City with businesses and residents' homes on either side of the road. She'd seen the sign: Population 2,383. All that meant to her was more trouble. "Damn it!" she said, slamming her fist against the steering wheel and looking at the gas gauge again. They only had a quarter of a tank left.

Landon dug into the glove box and fished out a map. He retrieved a flashlight from his bag and washed the light over the map. "We could go up 167 towards Grayson."

"That's way off the beaten path. Besides, we would still have to go through here to reach the turnoff."

Beth squinted at the roadblock. It didn't look as if anyone was manning it, in fact they had yet to see a single soul.

"Well one thing's for sure, we can't just wait here. If you're right, those assholes won't be that far behind us. So what's it gonna be?" Landon asked before scoffing. "I can't believe I'm asking an eighteen-year-old what to do."

She turned in her seat. "Why do you have such a problem with that?"

"Because I'm older. Generally speaking, adults are supposed to have more experience. And yet back there, it was you thinking on your feet not me." He looked toward the sky. "Up there. That's me. I know what to do but down here, I'm just fumbling through life."

Beth had a sense there was more to what he was saying than just what they'd been through. There was no time to get into it. They needed to make a decision and fast. She touched her finger on the map. "Here are our options. We either go back to Forge Creek Road and around but that's going to add hours onto our time and there is a chance we might run into Lilith, or we dump this Jeep now and head into Mountain City by foot but we will be on the road for at least another five hours. Can you handle that?"

"After what we've just been through, I think so," he said nodding.

She killed the engine and hopped out, taking a knife and slashing two of the tires. There was no point in giving them an advantage. "That settles it. No going back now." They shrugged into their backpacks and trudged toward the blockade. Nearby they saw the remnants of a plane that had torn through a section of town and exploded upon impact into a thousand pieces of metal. Many of the buildings had been reduced to rubble, or were boarded up with signs on the front that read: YOU ENTER, YOU DIE!

"Friendly place," Landon said.

Beth squinted, staying alert for any movement. "Castine. Is it like this?"

"Small, you mean?"

"Yeah."

"I guess."

"You like living there?" Beth asked without even looking at him.

"No. I wanted to move to Florida but Sara wanted to stay close to home, and family."

"Makes sense."

"But I'm her family," he said.

"Parents are important," she replied, keeping an arrow taut in her bow. "They aren't here forever." They didn't walk straight up South Church Street but went around the back of the buildings, stopping at the corners to make sure it was clear before darting to the next one.

"That's what she said," Landon replied. They got close

to a gas station called the Lazy Day Market. "I'm starting to think we could have moved some of those vehicles out of the way and driven through here. Where is everyone?"

Even though Mountain City was considered a small town, it wasn't so small that people would have had to leave. There was plenty of woodland, wildlife and streams to support a basic way of life. It was late at night so perhaps residents were sleeping but something seemed very odd.

"There should be someone patrolling like they were in Ryerson," Beth said.

Landon was just about to dart from the gas station over to an Amish furniture store when Beth spotted two men stepping out of a building across the street. She clasped the back of Landon's jacket and pulled him back behind cover. Without saying a word she indicated with a hand gesture to the men. They were both armed with rifles slung over their shoulders. One lit a cigarette and blew gray smoke into the air. They were talking but they were too far away to make out what they were saying.

A door opened and the sound of music drifted out. It sounded like someone playing a guitar, and a fiddle. Another guy joined them holding a bottle of beer in his hand. They were discussing something when the rumble of engines caught Beth's attention. She moved along the back of the car wash facility and saw multiple motorbikes roaring up the road. Under the glow of the moon she recognized one of them — Ruby. *Shit.* Her mind shifted into overdrive. Where the hell had they got those from? She was certain there were no bikes out front. *Maybe out back. Damn it!*

Beth hurried back to where Landon was crouched at the corner of the building. "We need to get out of here and fast. They're here." No sooner had she said that than the bikes roared into view carving up the road and pulling up outside a bar near to the three men. All of them had their guns raised, ready for trouble.

"Wait," Landon said as Beth tried to pull him east towards the tree line. They watched as Ruby slipped off a large motorcycle and looked around. She approached one of the men without any fear and slapped the barrel of the bearded guy's rifle out of her face. She strolled straight past him and walked into the bar while the others waited outside.

"Landon. We need to move."

He nodded and followed her, staying low to the ground. They darted through a dense grove of spindly trees into a residential area. A large rottweiler barked and it was then Beth stopped jogging. "Grizzly." She suddenly realized in all the commotion that she'd forgotten him. She figured he was with Landon.

"Grizzly. Oh my God. I've gotta go back."

"What?" he said grabbing her by the arm as she turned to head back.

"He was with you. I saw them take him into the restaurant."

Then just like that it dawned on him. In their fear, confusion and hurry to escape they had left him behind. She couldn't believe it. That dog was like a shadow. Very rarely did she need to tell him to follow as he was always there, at her side. But under duress her mind had slipped.

"Beth, we can't go back. First, it's too risky, and second, we drove here. That has to be at least a two-hour hike. I'm sorry but you've got to leave him."

Her brow furrowed. "Leave him? I'm not leaving my dog."

Landon stared back at her in disbelief. She didn't expect him to understand but Grizzly was the only family she had left. She berated herself as she trudged back through the trees cursing under her breath. How could she be so stupid? Landon soon caught up with her. "Beth. Look, I get it. I do. And under any other circumstances I would be right there with you but you saw those women. They are searching for us, and that Jeep back there has flat tires."

"I did what was right at the time."

Decisions to survive weren't always black and white. If her father had taught her anything, it was that life was fluid not rigid, and the only way to overcome obstacles was to be fluid, adapting to situations on the fly.

She stopped walking and placed a hand on a tree trunk as tears welled up.

Since everything had happened, she hadn't had time to process it. It had been one thing to the next without a moment to breathe. Even when she was looking after Landon for those four months, her mind was on protecting the cabin, making sure they had enough to eat and drink. And now this. It was all too much.

Landon placed a hand on her shoulder. "It's okay."

"No it's not. I'm going back. You should wait here."

"And do what?"

"I don't know, Landon. But I screwed this up. I need to fix it. It will be faster if I go by myself." She couldn't believe they had only made it to Mountain City. If the rest of the journey to Maine was like this, they would be lucky to survive. She broke into a run leaving him behind, her mind fixed on only one thing — getting Grizzly back.

Chapter 8

"She's dead?" Sara asked. They'd stepped outside to keep the conversation private. While Sam knew rumors had already spread about the recent string of murders, he didn't want everyone asking too many questions. Right now he was searching for answers, giving the incident his due diligence and hoping, no, scratch that, praying that someone had at bare minimum witnessed something.

"Unfortunately."

Although Castine was a small town and he knew many of the locals, it had taken the events at the start of the blackout to give him reason to meet her. Sara wrapped her arms around her body to keep herself warm. She was wearing an oversized gray windbreaker, jeans, a white sweater and knee-high brown boots. Under the glow of the moon he noticed how attractive she was. "And you think it had something to do with those three that attacked me?"

He raised his eyebrows. "I'm not saying that. We're exploring options. Those three were from out of town. I think they saw an opportunity and took it." He rested his hand on his duty belt and looked out into the darkness. It was still cold but nowhere near what they'd experienced in the winter. Spring in Maine was usually wet. The stately elm trees that towered over properties were beginning to green and temperatures were moderate. "I just want to know if you may have heard or seen anything unusual. The victim was shot twice. I thought you might be able to shed some light on the victim."

Mary Cline was a single woman who owned a herbal store in town. A nice woman in her forties, she kept to herself and owned an apartment above the store. Sara would often see her out jogging in the early hours of the morning. She was big on looking after the mind, body and soul, and once a month she ran a yoga workshop at the community center.

"No, I'm sorry. She used to jog by here but that's it. Was she in running gear?" Sara asked.

"I'm not at liberty to say right now."

"Deputy."

"Call me Sam."

"Sam, I think we're a little beyond the point of regular policing, don't you think?"

He cocked his head. She was right. It was a habit. It wasn't like the information was going to jeopardize the case. "She was in jogging gear. Yes."

"Was anything stolen?"

"From her apartment? Yes, it was ransacked. Shelves emptied."

"And the other two women?"

"We haven't found them but their homes were looted."

"So you think whoever is doing this is targeting single women?"

He breathed in the crisp evening air. "It looks that way."

"Just out of curiosity. Are women the only ones that are being murdered?"

"No. There are others but…"

"You're not at liberty to say."

"Some things we need to keep to ourselves," he said.

She nodded. "I wish I could help you but I don't know anything. Mary was a good woman. I couldn't imagine her withholding from anyone who asked." Sara ran a hand over her face. "You wouldn't have heard any news about my husband and daughter, would you?"

"No. We've been too busy trying to work out the fine details of deputizing locals in town."

She gave a slow nod. "Is it only supplies that are taken?"

"We're still trying to determine that."

Sara shifted her weight from one foot to the next. "Why are you doing this?"

"What?"

"It's been four months and you're still giving your time to policing."

"Someone has to maintain order."

"Have you seen it out there? It's far from orderly."

Sam leaned against a post. "I'm a realist, Mrs. Gray, I—"

"Call me Sara."

"Sara it is. Listen, right now I don't think we can stop crime from occurring, at least the kind of crime that is happening because of the blackout, but we can show up, walk the streets and that often can be a deterrent for those thinking of committing crime. As for these women. Well, I think the three are connected and someone or some group is responsible. It's my job to find out who."

"Well I appreciate you stopping by."

He turned to walk away. "I see Jake and Rita have moved in. Tess too?"

"Not yet."

He smiled. "You seem to be building your own small community."

"Best to stick together, don't you think, Sam?"

He nodded. "Well if anything comes to mind, drop by Emerson Hall. It's being used as a central base for our operations. Though I'm not there very often, but you can always leave a message with Clara, she's the administrator."

Sam called out to Carl who was inside having a drink. He bid farewell and came out to the vehicle they'd commandeered from a resident in Hancock County. It was a brown Toyota Land Cruiser J40 with a white roof. An ugly beast but as long as it ran, it didn't matter. They'd used white paint to put the word Police on the front and both sides so people knew.

"Any luck?" Carl asked as he fired up the vehicle and backed out.

"Nothing."

"I told you it was pointless. No one will say anything even if they were a witness. People are too afraid and they know we just don't have the manpower."

They drove back to Emerson Hall with the intention of checking in with Clara to see if those they were meant to deputize had shown up. It was supposed to be done earlier that morning but Bud Stephens and Jillian White had been a no show. They'd driven over to their residences but didn't get an answer when they knocked. The decision to deputize them hadn't come without some backlash from the community. Not everyone was in favor of having Stephens or White involved.

Stephens was an old-timer in his late fifties who had military experience but had been out of the military for over twenty-eight years. Partially retired, he offered his services as a charter fisherman. However, while his career track record was flawless, his personal life had left something to be desired. It seemed he'd been charged with assault before he moved to Castine, something that only a few locals who drank at the same bar with him were aware of.

White also had a marred past. She'd served as an auxiliary police officer in New York for a few years until her family moved north and she had become a therapist. The trouble was some of the advice she'd given had led to one of her clients committing suicide.

Teresa McKenna, Castine's town manager, was involved in the vetting process and somehow those snippets of information had been left out of the applications. Upon announcing who would be deputized at a town hall meeting, it was the locals who had brought these overlooked issues to light. Still, regardless of their past they were the only ones in town that had any experience that would be of use to them.

Though now he was starting to wonder if someone had scared them off.

"What about Sara? We could deputize her," Carl said.

"Don't be stupid."

"I'm not. Name one woman in this town who can handle three thugs."

"First, I can't. Second, I don't think she handled all three of them. Someone helped her. I think she's covering for them."

"Jake, you mean?"

"Jake. Max. Hell, even Rita."

"Rita Thompson. Now there's a deputy if I've ever seen one." Carl roared with laughter.

"Oh yeah, that's a real knee slapper," Sam said.

"What's up your ass?"

Sam groaned. "It just pisses me off that someone is out there killing these women and they'll probably do it again and we haven't got a damn clue. It makes us look like imbeciles. I saw the way Sara looked at me like I was out of my mind."

Carl cast a sideways glance. "Oh I see how it is. I tell you it's insane to be doing this and you shoot me down, but she tells you and you're all up in arms."

He shrugged. "It's a matter of respect."

"What, you don't respect my opinion?" Carl asked.

"It's not like that. I mean..." He trailed off but couldn't exactly put it into words. As they came around the bend on La Tour Street, which intersected with Perkins Street, Sam eased off the gas. Up ahead a crowd had gathered at the end of a driveway. "What the heck is going on here?" he said before swerving to the edge of the road as a man came charging towards them waving his hands. Before he could get out the man was at his window banging on it.

Sam brought it down as the man pointed to the end of the road. "A guy broke into my neighbor's house and beat her unconscious. I think he would have dragged her away had it not been for me. He's taken off on foot. A couple of my boys have gone after him."

"Carl, go check on the woman while I…"

"Why don't you do that?"

"Carl."

He groaned. "Okay. Okay."

He hopped out and Sam asked for directions. The man pointed and Sam slammed his foot against the pedal, veered off the road and cut through a grove of trees. He bounced in his seat as the Toyota roared over a rough terrain and smashed through branches blocking his path. It burst out into a clearing and he spotted the two young guys barreling toward a heavily forested area not far from the Wilson Museum. Sam took the magnet-mounted emergency light and put it on top of the Toyota. It flashed wildly and the two teens, who were carrying baseball bats, pointed. He glanced ahead just in time to see a figure dart into the tree line. *Shit.* He powered the vehicle past the boys trying to keep control of it over the uneven ground. Getting closer to the tree line he swerved and shut the engine off. He took the keys to avoid someone stealing it, and bounced out of the vehicle with his service weapon drawn. He clicked the light on top of the weapon on and shone it into the dark woods.

Running in without backup went against his better judgment but the chance of this being the same individual who'd taken the other three women was too good to pass up. He pressed on, darting around trees and scanning the thick underbrush. Under a canopy of green leaves it was hard to see anything except the silhouette of trunks, branches and underbrush. He stopped and listened, his chest rising and falling hard as he tried to catch his breath. Up ahead, slightly off to his left he heard the swish of pants.

Sam took off in that direction, his mind ran amuck. What if there was more than one? What if they were armed? The thought of being shot was always at the forefront of his mind as an officer but that's what he'd signed up for.

No sooner had he thought that than a round snapped past him and tore into a tree. Slamming into a tree he took cover, his gun raised near his face. He peered around the tree trying to get a bead on the gunman. Nothing.

Sam dropped to the ground and picked up a stone the size of a baseball and tossed it a few feet away. Another round erupted. The gunman was waiting for him to step out. Slowing his breathing he repeated the same action again, this time he waited until the round sounded before he shot out in the other direction, scanning the trees and hurrying to take cover behind another tree. "I've got you," he muttered under his breath. The gunman was crouched behind a tree, twenty yards away.

There was no point telling him the gig was up as that would only give away his location and no one with a gun under these circumstances would willingly lay it down and hand themselves in. He knew this was a life or death moment.

Sam snuck another peek and nearly had his face shot off. He felt the wind as the bullet slipped past his cheek. His stomach caught in his throat as he unleashed three rounds and raced forward. He squeezed off another two and tried to close the distance between them.

Turning to get another look, he heard a rustle above and looked up just in time to see a mound of black drop onto him. His gun flew out of his hand and he felt two fists pummel him from behind. Although he tried to get up, his attacker had his knee dug into his back and an arm around his throat.

"Get his gun," a young voice cried out. Sam tried to see what was happening but every time he turned his face, a fist struck him. "Kill him."

"No, he's a cop," another male voice said.

"It doesn't matter."

The conversation between the two of them was odd, like a power struggle between one who wanted to be there and the other who was just along for the ride. "You kill me, you will..." Before Sam could get the words out, he was knocked unconscious.

* * *

When he came to, he found Carl snapping fingers in front of his face. "Hey buddy. Sam. You with me?"

"Where are they?"

"They?"

"There were two of them."

"You were knocked unconscious. Luckily, Tom Riddling's boys found you. Who knows what could have happened." The left side of Sam's face was badly swollen, his jaw ached, and he could taste iron in his mouth. "Here, take a drink of this," Carl said bringing up a metal can to his mouth. He lifted his head back and swallowed then coughed hard. It was whiskey. "Good stuff, huh?"

Sam went to get up but staggered.

"Whoa, slow it down. You took one hell of a beating."

Nearby were Tom Riddling's two teenage sons, Greg and Niles. They were glancing around the woodland. Tom owned a fabrication shop and his boys were set to take it over. "Did you ask them if they can ID the two who got away?"

"No. However Greg said he got a good look at one of them. Said he was male, white, couldn't have been older than nineteen."

"There were two of them, Carl. Both were young. If Greg's right, we're looking for teenagers. Fucking teenagers!" he said running a hand over his face. How could they be responsible for the disappearance of women and the death of one? What was this town coming to? He rubbed his face. "How's the woman?" he asked.

"She'll live. But she took one hell of a beating. I'm sure if Tom hadn't come along, she would have died." Sam crouched and squeezed the bridge of his nose, wiping blood away with the back of his arm. They might not have a name or a face but at least they had a profile and that was something.

Chapter 9

The woman's mouth opened to cry out but nothing escaped her lips. Beth tore the jagged knife out from underneath her jaw and released the woman's body. She slumped to the ground and Beth fished into her pockets for the keys to the motorcycle. She straddled the green Harley Davidson MT350E and brought it to life, all the while eyeing the door to the bar.

It was all about timing.

She'd crouched in the shadows and watched the rabble of women stream into the bar, leaving two outside. She'd taken out the first with an arrow on the west side of the bar and crept up behind the second on the east side.

Beth powered on, and powered up the bike. She was certain the roar would bring them out. She'd expected to be chased but it never happened. Releasing the clutch slowly and giving it gas, she jerked forward out of the lot and tore away while looking back in the side mirror to see if anyone was coming out of the bar. The gasoline fumes were dizzying combined with the adrenaline pumping through her as she veered around abandoned vehicles. The bike rattled between her legs, and she squeezed the clutch again, shifting it up another gear.

Landon was right, walking from Mountain City to the Neva Grill would have taken two hours, that's why she'd opted for the bike which would reduce the time to less than fifteen minutes. If she was honest, she was flying by the seat of her pants, making split-second decisions in the heat of the moment. That was never good when it came to survival but remaining fluid kept her mind clear as she flipped on the headlight. A beam shot out lighting up the curves of the road.

Beth's heart thumped in her chest as she thought about the risk she was taking. Landon didn't understand. Those who'd never owned a dog wouldn't. The bond between her and Grizzly was like concrete. That dog had been with her through the worst and there was no way in hell she was leaving him behind. A slip of the mind under duress was forgivable, but purposely walking away from family, nope. And that's what he was — family.

Focus.

Stay focused, she told herself.

How the hell would she get back to Landon? She couldn't exactly put Grizzly on the back of a bike. *What are you doing, Beth? Why are you going to all this trouble for this man?* She couldn't answer that. It wasn't because he didn't know how to survive, it was because she couldn't stay on that mountain. Not at the cabin. Not anywhere it would remind her of her parents. She needed a fresh start, somewhere new and figured Maine was as good as any other place.

She shifted through the gears; third, fourth, and felt the smoothness of the road beneath the tires. The wind whistled in her ears making her eyes water.

At the first sign for the Neva Grill, Beth pulled off the road and hid the bike in the underbrush. She pulled the SIG and hurried through the dense woods toward the rear. Lights were shining out through the windows. How many were left? There had been at least ten women that had arrived in Mountain City by bike. Beth circled around the restaurant staying in the darkness, her eyes washing over the women. *Okay. Where are you? Where are you keeping him?* She spotted the generator out back, churning away, and an idea came to her. Pitching sideways down a steep incline, Beth hurried; loose rocks rolled down ahead of her. Her throat burned from breathing so hard as she made her way over to the generator and shut it off. She went a step further and took a knife and cut one of the cables behind the side panel.

She then hurried back into the shadows and waited.

Having all the lights go out got an instant response. Two women came out, one holding a rifle and scanning the tree line as the other jogged over to the generator. Beth already had an arrow prepared. She aimed at the chest of the woman who was watching the other one's back and unleashed it. It hit with pinpoint accuracy downing her. The other girl turned her head but before she could react, Beth came out of the tree line with an arrow pointed at her. "Say a word and I drop you." She dashed forward. "Do as I say and you will live." She hurried over. "Get on your knees now."

The girl complied; fear masked her face. She wasn't much older than Beth. How Lilith had managed to reel in so many young girls was mind-boggling. She came up behind her and shoved her to the ground and then placed the arrow against the back of her head so she could feel the tip. "Where is my dog?"

"In the restaurant."

"Have you hurt him?"

"No. We're not like that."

"Look, all I want is my dog and I'm out of here."

"You won't be able to get him without going through us."

She gritted her teeth. She was more than prepared to burn the whole fucking place down if she had to but with her dog inside, that was out of the question.

"Why did you kill Willow?" the girl asked.

"She gave me no other choice."

The words seemed unreal to her but yet it was the truth. Beth looked towards the restaurant. "You probably have a few minutes to let me get this generator back on or others will come out looking for us."

"Is that so?" Beth muttered, her mind going through her options.

She looked at what the girl was wearing. All of them were dressed in tight black gear with anoraks that had hoods to cover their face. It was a long shot but she had to try it. It was pitch dark without the lights; how would they know any different?

"Take your clothes off."

"What?"

Beth pushed the arrow hard against her head. "Hurry."

She removed her foot from her back and the girl stripped out of her gear. Beth then took out some rope from her backpack. She forced the girl down and hog tied her. She then took a piece of cloth and stuck it into her mouth. Just as she did that, someone called out. "Hey Rebecca. What's taking so long?" Shit. Beth loomed over the girl expecting someone to approach. *Think fast.* She told the girl what to say and removed the rag with the threat of killing her if she said any different.

"Just a few minutes longer," Rebecca cried out while eyeing Beth.

"Good job. You get to live." Immediately Beth shoved the cloth back into her mouth and hurried towards the restaurant. She left her bow in a bush and pulled up the hood, keeping her hand on a knife as she approached the side door. It was so dark inside that as she opened the door no one even noticed. They were moaning about power, discussing the attack on the guy and her and all manner of things as she slipped through them unnoticed, her hood up, cloaked by darkness. Her eyes scanned looking for Grizzly. *Where are you?* She let out a low whistle that only he was familiar with and heard the sound of paws scratching against a door. The bastards had put him in the washroom and put a chair in front of it so the dog couldn't get out.

"Someone want to see what's holding things up? Fuck

sake!" a girl yelled. "I swear we need to select smarter women. The last batch have been awful."

Time was ticking. She knew it was only a matter of minutes before the one pushing through the crowd heading for the door would find the two women. Beth made her way over to the washroom and was close to reaching the door when she bumped shoulders with a woman. "Hey, mind where you're going."

Keeping her head down she replied, "Sorry."

The girl looked at her and placed a hand on her shoulder. "Do I…"

Before she finished, Beth drove a knife into her gut and leaned against her while moving forward. She dropped her behind the restaurant counter and continued on. She expected someone saw her but in the darkness all of them were nothing but silhouettes.

As soon as she reached the door, she opened it and clasped Grizzly's collar.

"What are you doing with the dog?" someone said behind her.

"Lilith wants me to take it out before it craps on the floor. Now get the fuck out of my way," she said. The girl stepped aside as she led the dog out the front of the restaurant. All the while her heart was hammering in her chest, certain that someone would stop her. But no one did.

Beth made her way around to collect the bow but then all hell broke loose.

The woman sent outside to check on Rebecca came rushing back, nearly slamming into her on the way. She took one glance at the dog and looked at Beth. "Sic 'em," Beth said to Grizzly. He knew the command. He hadn't been trained to harm humans but after the way he'd been treated, he knew who was the enemy. Grizzly launched in the air, knocking the girl over, and tore at her neck. Beth hurried over and collected her arrow just in time to see some of the women come out. She had no choice but to engage. She unleashed two arrows, back to back, both hitting their mark as she let out a whistle. "Grizzly. Let's go."

The dog spat some bloodied flesh and bounded after her. They hurried up an incline as rounds whistled behind them tearing into the trees.

Beth swallowed hard.

Now they were the hunted.

* * *

Eight miles away, Landon reached into his pocket for the unopened packet of cigarettes. He had taken cover inside the cab of an eighteen-wheeler in some business lot. He wasn't far away from where Beth had left him. He didn't want to stray just in case she returned and couldn't find him. Landon stared at the pack. "Screw it!" He unwrapped them and pulled one out, quickly lighting it and inhaling deeply. *Oh my God, that's good.* Then seconds after came the familiar guilt. He'd managed to go months without having one because of his injury. That was the longest amount of time without a cigarette. Sara would have been ecstatic. But all this had worn him down. How stupid he was to think they could make it a thousand miles across the country without issue. They hadn't even made it to the Appalachian Trail. He brought a hand up to his head and leaned back in the passenger side of the cab. What had become of the country? At one time Americans would have stood shoulder to shoulder and helped one another but now he didn't know who to trust.

Staring west down Depot Street he watched as the group of women on bikes barreled north on Old School Street searching for Beth. He'd seen her kill the two women and head south out of town. He had to keep reminding himself that she was eighteen. In some ways he felt sorry for her; having to kill to survive. All of this was his fault. Not the event but the situation. Had he not encouraged her to come with him, they wouldn't be here. He was beginning to think that maybe he should go on without her. If she returned, she'd find him gone and maybe she would go back to her cabin. They weren't that far away that she couldn't change her mind.

The nicotine finally hit his system, calming his nerves. He pulled out the map and shone a light on it. He knew where they were and Beth had already drawn out the direction they would head in but he wanted to see what route he would need to take. He hated hiking. Any long-distance walking for that matter. He could never understand the fascination with trudging through the wilderness. It was dangerous. Full of bugs that carried Lyme disease and animals that could tear you apart. Oh there might be some nice waterfalls, or cool views, but could it come close to being thousands of feet in the air? At least up there he was in control, or at least he thought he was.

Go on without her, he told himself. She'll be better for it.

He wrestled in his mind, tossed up about continuing on or waiting.

Even if by a slim chance she managed to get Grizzly, how the hell could she make it back on that bike? *Just face the facts. She's gone.* He then started to think that maybe she wanted it that way. A reason to leave him. Who wouldn't? He deserved this. Over and over he punished himself with his mind. Tearing away what was good.

It was settled. He would continue on without her.

Landon took the last few drags of his cigarette then hopped out of the cab and stubbed it out. He blew smoke in the air, shrugged the bag into a comfortable position on his back and kept a firm grip on the Smith & Wesson revolver.

Staying low and making sure to avoid the main veins of the town he pressed on parallel to Depot Street, sticking to the back of buildings and the closest tree line.

He hurried upon hearing the roar of motorcycles.

Landon had made it to the animal clinic on the corner of Depot and Main Street when he saw four of the women coming his way. He pulled back and looked around for somewhere to hide, taking cover between two vehicles. The bikes growled past and he held his breath, expecting to be found. Crouched behind a vehicle, he heard a whistle.

He turned to his left but didn't see anything, then he heard it again. This time he noticed a guy looking out of a window motioning him over. Landon pointed to himself and he nodded. "Hurry."

At first, he was hesitant and would have ignored him and continued on but the rumble of bikes coming back again gave him no other option. They were sweeping the streets searching for them. Landon darted into a darkened side door at the clinic.

"How many are out there?" a guy said bringing a flashlight up to his face. He was a scrawny man wearing a baseball cap on back to front, a dirty jean jacket and jeans with holes in them. He was sporting a goatee and had a patch on the back of the jacket.

"What?"

"Reapers."

"Who?"

"The bike gang that has this town by the balls."

"You mean the women?"

"No," he said. Frustrated, he turned and shone his flashlight on his back. It lit up a patch of a Grim Reaper riding a motorbike with a sickle in hand.

"You with them?"

He chuckled. "No. I stole this off the guy I killed. Figured I could use it to get out of here." Landon offered a puzzled look. The guy attempted to clarify. "How many people do you see on the streets?"

"None, except the women."

"Exactly. These assholes drove them out a few months back. Killed a whole bunch of people," he said looking out a window and then back at him. "You got any food on you?"

"Yeah." He took off his backpack and fished out a bag of jerky and tossed it to him.

"Ah sweet." The guy tucked into it like a ravenous beast.

Landon studied him. "When was the last time you ate anything?"

"Two days ago." He pulled another chunk out and downed it before handing it back. "Here."

"You're hungry. Right?"

"Yeah but I don't want to eat everything you got

unless..."

"Go ahead, I've got more."

"Really?" He sounded as if he had won the jackpot.

"What's your name?" Landon asked.

"Denzel."

Landon nodded. "Oh."

"What?"

"Nothing. It's just..."

"It's a black name?" Denzel replied.

Landon nodded.

"And?"

He pointed at him. "You're white."

"Very observant of you." He paused. "You racist?"

Landon balked. "No. God no. I have lots of friends who are black. I'm just saying."

He laughed and slapped Landon on the arm, moving over to another window. "I'm joking, man. My mother was a big fan of the actor. It's a nickname given to me." He extended his hand. "The name's Robbie Holmes but most call me Denzel."

"Why?"

He looked back at Landon with a confused expression and then dropped a few bars of a rap which completely caught him off guard. "It's my rapper name. You know, like Drake, Eminem, NF, Jay Z."

"But Denzel's an actor."

"Exactly. No one in the rap game goes by that name."

"I'm pretty sure someone does," Landon said rolling his eyes as he brushed past him, finding the guy a little odd. "Anyway, what are you doing in here?"

"What do you think? Staying alive!"

Chapter 10

The silhouette of figures. Voices.

Beth reacted immediately. She could hear the swish of pants pushing through the underbrush. They were hunting her and there were too many for her to kill.

Nerves on edge, she could hear them getting closer. She charged through the forest, leaping over debris, roots and downed trees. Her body was being eaten alive by bugs. Her biggest fear was that Grizzly would try to defend her and go after them and get shot. The motorcycle came to mind but slinging a ninety-pound German shepherd over it wasn't just impossible, it was ludicrous. No, she had to hope she could outrun them, or find somewhere she could hunker down and hide until they gave up the chase.

The church.

She'd recalled seeing another church about a mile down the road. If she could reach that, just maybe they could stay out of sight until morning. Stomach acid splashed up into her throat causing it to burn as she sprinted through the forest heading for a clearing. "C'mon, boy! Focus!" she said as Grizzly kept looking back and growling. Beth emerged from the tree line into an open field.

Exposed.

Out in full view, Beth stole a glance, ever aware that all it would take was one bullet to end her life. In those brief few seconds as she raced across the field, she wondered why it had come to this. Of course she understood why they were after her but she meant the blackout, her parents' death, Landon's plane crashing. It had to mean something, didn't it? Life wasn't just some random game, was it? Beth slapped away the questions. There would be time for them later, if she lived long enough. The church was located behind some homes off Fire Tower Road, a narrow path that curled into the hillside. An air of desperation smothered Beth's courage as she looked back and saw the group of women hurrying across the field.

She'd been spotted. Hurrying around to the front of the one-story church building she yanked on the door and was surprised to find it open. "Inside," she said to Grizzly. The dog shot in, sensing her urgency.

As they burst through, an older man dressed in a blue plaid shirt and jeans was kneeling at the altar, head lowered. He wheeled his head around bringing up a handgun towards them. Grizzly growled but Beth hushed him.

They stared at each other for a second as if he was trying to determine her intentions. Out of breath, her chest rose and fell. Beyond the walls they heard yelling, and someone shouting, "Which way did she go?"

Beth's eyes darted back to the man. "We just need somewhere to hide. Please."

Whether it was fate, an act of God or the kindness of a stranger, the man beckoned Beth to the back of the church. He led her to the back of the small stage at the front of the church, and behind a curtain. There he flipped back some old dirty carpet and yanked on a wooden door. Underneath it were steps that went down into darkness. A second of hesitation and then the sound of women's voices and she guided Grizzly down. "Don't say a word. Stay very quiet," he said closing the door above her and placing the carpet back over. Within seconds of him doing that, she heard a door burst open and boots enter the sanctuary.

"Pastor Michaels." The voice of Ruby echoed. "I would have thought by now you would have closed your doors forever. Not too many families around here in need of your services."

"God's doors are always open."

"God's doors." She roared with laughter. "I like that."

Inside the cramped space it was dark and smelled musty. Before she'd entered, she'd seen the faint silhouette of boxes. She figured it was being used for storage.

Only the sound of boots could be heard as if the women were searching the building. "A girl came this way only a few minutes ago. She wouldn't have come through

God's doors, would she?" she asked in a condescending way.

"It's just me."

"Just you. And the Lord of course. Don't forget the Lord, right?"

"Right," he replied. "What's this girl done?" he asked.

"Oh you know, wicked things. Sinful things. The kinds of things that require punishment. The Lord believes in punishment, doesn't he, pastor? He is a God of justice, is he not?"

"So you were listening."

Ruby laughed. "I remember a few things, and some others. Like that guy that worked in your children's church. What was his name? Ronald McKay. Wasn't that it, girls? Yeah, I'm sure that was it. Oh McKay loved to play."

"That was a long time ago."

"Yeah. Everything he did was brushed under the rug, wasn't it, pastor? Kept on the downlow. Oh, don't want to offend the parishioners, do we? That could lead to people shunning the church, and God forbid that should ever happen. Why, that could lead to people leaving, which would mean less money in your pocket, isn't that right?"

"Lilith and I have an agreement," the pastor said.

As soon as he spoke the words, Beth's heart sank. She'd just walked into the lion's den. She kept a firm hand over Grizzly's mouth to prevent him from making a noise. She whispered in his ear to stay quiet. One thing her father had done right was train Grizzly from a young age to obey commands.

"Yes. An agreement. How lucky you are to have her blessing. Pity McKay didn't have it. It's strange, when we visited him last month he no longer wanted to play. I mean, wouldn't you...now that we are grown up and have filled out? What do you think, pastor?"

Beth could only guess what she was showing him.

"Any luck, girls?" Ruby asked.

"Nothing."

"Well, looks like you're telling the truth, pastor. That

would be a first, now wouldn't it?"

More silence followed. Beth swallowed hard, beads of sweat dripping down her temple. She didn't need to imagine what they would do to her if they found her.

"You mind me asking why you're looking for this girl?"

"I just told you!" she said in a booming voice. "Sins, father. Sins. But don't worry, we'll be sure to make sure that justice is served. Come on girls, let's go." Boots scuffing the wooden floor, a door opening and closing then quiet. No movement at all. It remained that way for what felt like another ten minutes before the pastor pulled back the carpet and let her out.

"Come on out, they're gone. You should be safe now."

"Thank you," she said crawling out of the stifling hole. The pastor ran his hand over the dog and patted his back. Beth crossed to a window and looked out, still nervous they were out there.

"You want to tell me what you did to poke Lilith's brood of vipers?" he asked. Beth stole a glance over her shoulder.

"If you'll tell me why they let you live. I mean with her love for men and all."

He smirked and nodded. He ran his hand over a thick gray beard.

"My wife and I fostered Lilith before she left the system and turned into the person she's become today."

"Ah, so that explains the agreement," Beth said crossing the room to check the other side. It was hard to tell if they were still out there. It was quiet but that didn't mean they weren't lurking in the shadows waiting for her to show her face.

The pastor crouched beside Grizzly who seemed to know he was a good person as he rubbed his head against the man's leg. "The agreement is for me only. It didn't prevent her from killing my son."

"She killed your son?"

"And many others' sons." He shook his head. "This blackout was the opportunity she wanted. Sad, isn't it? That seemingly good people can change on a dime if presented with a chance to get away with murder."

"You're against murder then."

"God is, as such, so am I."

"Then you won't want to hear what I did," Beth said.

He rocked his head back. "Ah. I see."

"She didn't exactly give me any other option."

He nodded. "Yes." He breathed in deeply. "She has a way of getting under people's skin. You mind me asking who you killed?"

"Does it matter?"

He must have picked up the tone of her voice. "If I wanted to hand you over, I had my chance. Doing so now would only incriminate me."

"Several women. I don't know them. The only one that I had a name for was Willow."

His eyes widened. "Oh you've done it now."

"Why?"

"It doesn't matter. What matters is getting you away from here. A long way away."

"I was trying to do that but had to come back for my

dog."

He stared at her. "You came back and risked your life for your dog?"

"I know. Landon thought the same."

"Landon?"

"Ah, the guy I was with."

"Boyfriend? Father?"

"Neither. A friend I was helping get home."

"And where is this Landon?"

"Mountain City," she said.

He rose from stroking Grizzly and nodded. "There's only one place worse than here and that's there."

"Why?"

He frowned. "You're not from around here, are you?"

"No. The Blue Ridge Mountains." Her chest felt heavy as a wave of grief hit her. In the eighteen years she'd been alive, she'd only traveled through the mountains and her own town. There had never been any reason to go beyond that. Money had been tight so her parents didn't vacation like other families.

"A few months back a large biker gang rolled through here on their way to Mountain City. Killed a number of people. Good people. Many that were trying to rebuild and help the community. Anyway, they took up residence in Mountain City. They're bad news, that's all you need to know. If your friend is there let's hope he's still alive."

"I need to get there. You wouldn't have a working vehicle, would you?"

He chuckled. "No. But I do know someone who can get you there. C'mon, follow me." He headed toward the door and looked back. "By the way, I'm Jason. Jason Michaels, and you are?"

"Beth Sullivan. But my father called me Bluebird."

"What a beautiful name. Why Bluebird?" he asked as he cracked the door open and looked out into the darkness.

"It's a long story," she said. He didn't probe any further. "You think they're still out there?"

"Hard to know but we can't stay here. I'm sure Ruby will come back when she can't find you. That girl has a nose like a sniffer dog. She's a complete train wreck."

"Aren't you meant to have endless hope for the lost?"

He smiled. "God might, I don't." He gestured to her and they made a move, racing out of the church, across to his home where he collected a rifle and a flashlight and they took off on foot towards the woods. A part of her wanted to trust him but after everything that happened, she had her doubts. That's why she kept a firm grip on the SIG.

"You have family? I mean besides your son. A wife?" Beth asked.

"I did. Beautiful woman. Passed away from breast cancer a few years ago. Thankfully she didn't live long enough to see this new world."

The woods were dark and gloomy. Every shadow set Beth's nerves on edge. A few times, Jason told her to stop as if he thought they were being followed. Satisfied, they continued on.

"With Lilith in this community, and the bikers in the next. Why do you stick around?" Beth asked.

"To be a light in the darkness. There are some girls that visit me on a regular basis. Lilith knows and allows it. You see, Beth, while she has done some horrific things since the blackout, deep down inside of her I know there is good. Without me around maybe what little light is left will be swallowed by the darkness. So I stay."

"But how are you surviving?"

"Lilith. Crazy, right. The very person that has wreaked havoc on this community still shows mercy to me. I'm not sure why."

"Because you're a good person," Beth said.

He looked at her and smiled. "Believe me, I have made mistakes." He looked up into the sky as if knowing that God was looking down upon him. He didn't elaborate and she wouldn't pry. That was between him and his maker. She certainly wasn't one to judge.

They walked for close to ten minutes when they heard voices.

Jason grabbed her and pulled her back and they took cover in a dense grove of trees. Between the trees they saw

Ruby and the others speaking with someone near a house before they hurried away. They both waited there in silence for a few more minutes before reemerging.

Jogging the rest of the way, they made it to an old trailer on cement blocks with an aging Chevy truck out front. There appeared to be animal carcasses in the back of the truck covered by a tarp. Hooves stuck out at different angles.

Jason scanned the terrain before they approached the trailer.

He gave the door a hard knock and she heard someone inside curse.

It opened wide, a small light from a hand-crank flashlight lit up the face of a short man with a prosthetic arm. "What the…" His gaze washed over them. "Jason?"

"Gareth. I need your help. Can we come in?"

He nodded and waved them in. As soon as the door was closed the questions began.

"Who's this?" Gareth asked.

"A friend. Look, you're doing that run into Mountain

City tomorrow?"

"Yeah. And?"

"Can you deliver the goods sooner?"

"Why?"

"I need to get her back to her friend."

He stared at Beth and his lip curled up. "You're the one they're looking for, aren't you?"

"Is this going to be a problem?" Jason asked.

"It will be if I get caught with her."

"I'll deal with Lilith."

"It's not Lilith I'm worried about. It's Bosley."

Beth interjected. "Forget it. I don't want to cause any trouble."

"A little late for that, don't you think?" Gareth said. "You killed Willow."

"Okay, who is Willow?" This was the second time her name had been mentioned and she was beginning to think that she wasn't just one of the girls.

Jason looked as if he was about to tell her but Gareth beat him to the punch.

"She was Bosley's girl."

"And Bosley is?"

Gareth chuckled, a frown forming as if he was confused by the question. "Only the leader of the most dangerous biker gang in the region."

Chapter 11

Call it a stroke of luck or the power of a community that was tired of being victims but not long after the two intruders escaped, a witness had reported seeing two young males heading north. One of them was wearing a similar jacket to the guy who was seen at the house of the Riddlings' neighbor. Using some street smarts, the witness had followed from a distance on a bicycle and observed them entering a home just south of Castine Cemetery.

"Are you sure?" Sam asked, still nursing a swollen eye. He held a bag of ice against his face. It soothed and numbed his face making it feel good after ten minutes. Without power the regular way of making ice wasn't available to them but Rodney Jennings, a local university student, had come up with a way using equal parts water and acetone in a cup. Sam had never seen how he did it but it involved a bell jar and a vacuum pump powered by solar. In fact if he hadn't seen the final ice with his own eyes, he wouldn't have believed it was possible. Anyway, the kid was making a killing creating ice for people to keep their fish fresh. He'd already worked out a few deals whereby he didn't have to go fishing at all, there were those who gave him a cut of their catch.

Carl nodded. "Seems so. You know State Street?"

"Yep."

"Okay, so you come off that instead of going left on Windmill Hill Lane, and then you take a right. That narrow road heads up to the cemetery but on the right is a home."

"With a pool. I know it. Jenn Whitfield lives there."

Their eyes went wide and both of them said at the same time, "She's single."

Not missing a beat, Sam tossed the ice and thanked the Riddling's and headed for their Jeep. "I'm coming with you," Tom said.

"Tom. Let us handle it."

"You don't know how many are in there. Besides, it wasn't your neighbor who got sucker punched in the face.

That could have been my wife. Just give me a second to grab my rifle."

Sam looked at Carl and he shrugged. Under any other conditions they would have stopped him but with those they were meant to deputize not showing up and only themselves policing the small town, he figured it was probably best they had some backup. "More eyes the better," Carl said.

Sam brought the vehicle up to Tom's house and watched as he told his sons to keep an eye on the house while he was away. His instructions were clear. "Anyone tries to break in, shoot them."

It was a new world they were living in. Sure, in the past, Americans had a right to protect their property but whereas before gun protesters might have been up in arms with Americans having access to weapons and being allowed to shoot at will, there wasn't anyone complaining now. Hell, if your neighbor had a gun it could be both intimidating or comforting depending on how well you got along with them before the blackout. The dynamics of society had changed. It was all about watching out for each other because if your neighbor wound up dead, there was a good chance you could.

Tom hopped in the back and began checking his rifle. Tom was a broad-shouldered man, six-foot, dirty blond hair that was almost gray and his skin looked as if it had been in the sun for too long. He was packing an AR-15. "I hope you boys have ballistic vests as you know how these things can play out."

"Tom, you sure you know how to shoot that?"

Tom burst out laughing. "Boy, I was shooting the wings off a fly when you were just a sperm cell in your daddy's ballbag." Amused, Carl nearly spat out his drink. "I did six years in the military."

As they swerved out onto Perkins Street, Sam frowned. "Military? But you were at the town hall meeting the other night. We asked for people to put their hands up if they had any military experience — yours was down."

"You're damn right it was. Time away to protect these clusterfucks on this island is time away from my family. I figured you would run me ragged. I've served my time."

"So why are you here now?"

"Because this shit happened on my doorstep," he said. "I want these assholes off the street just as bad as the rest of you but I'm not working eight hours a day, walking the streets like you idiots."

"Idiots, I told you," Carl said. "That's exactly what they think."

Sam rolled his eyes.

"No. With all respect I admire what you're trying to do and I'm sure it keeps the old-timers happy but I'm not a fool. One busted-up vehicle, two cops, please, it's like a bad cop movie from the '80s." Carl couldn't contain himself. He slapped his knee and roared with laughter. Meanwhile Tom sat in the back with a straight face. The guy was dead serious.

"Well just do me a favor and don't point that thing my way, okay," Sam said focusing on the road ahead.

"So what's the deal?" Tom asked. "Give it to me straight up. Not the politically correct version you told these brain-dead residents at the town hall meeting. Is the department defunct? Are we looking at mass genocide? Has the sheriff stepped down? And is FEMA really helping or are they enslaving us for some mass orgy? Because I swear heads are gonna roll if they try to take my gun."

"Oh my God," Sam said quietly under his breath. He was beginning to think it was a bad idea allowing him to tag along. "Look, just follow my lead and don't get too trigger happy. The last thing we need is more dead bodies."

They veered out of Pleasant Street and all three of them looked the picture of seriousness. There was no telling what they were walking into, whether it was just two teens or a group, and if it was a group, what were they willing to do to survive?

Sam parked in Eatons Lane and killed the engine. They hopped out and Sam went around back, slipped into a ballistic vest and donned a helmet he'd got for SWAT incidents. Carl did the same. He palmed a magazine into a carbine rifle and Carl loaded up his Mossberg 590A1 shotgun. Sam gave Tom strict instructions to wait at the end of the driveway. His job was simple: to stop them if they tried to escape on foot or via a vehicle while they moved in on the house.

"Oh yeah, give me the shit job."

"You're lucky you're even here," Sam said, throwing him a scowl.

"As if you could stop me," Tom said waiting for a response. Sam never replied. "I didn't think so." He jogged away.

"He's quite the character, isn't he?" Carl said, smirking as they ran at a crouch across an open area towards the trees that hedged in the property. Under the cover of darkness they navigated their way through the wooded area, traipsing over downed trees, and working their way through thick bushes of thorns. They passed by several homes. A few residents were outside. He raised a hand to them and told them to get inside. They didn't hesitate. When they reached an area where Jenn's home was visible, they could see the flicker of candles through the windows. Sam raised two fingers and pointed for Carl to go while he went around the pool to the side door.

He pulled the two-way radio off his hip and whispered into it, "What you got?"

"I've got two guys on the main floor, looks like there could be another on the second floor," Carl said as he came up the back towards the French doors.

"Keep those two in sight. I'm heading in. When shit flies, back me up."

"You know I always do," he muttered.

Sam looked off to his left and groaned. Coming through a heavily wooded area was Tom. Sam put a hand up and pursed his lips but the guy just kept coming. This was why the police weren't keen on just hiring anyone. Training was key. Following orders, golden.

"What are you doing?" Sam said in a hushed tone.

"I'm of no use to you down there. Don't worry, I won't steal the glory; I'll just stay over here. If they come out the front, I'll cut them down."

"You are not to fire unless fired upon."

"Are you kidding me?" Tom said. "These asshats aren't going to play nice. If you think you're gonna wander in there and have them lay down their guns after what they've committed, you're out of your mind."

"Tom."

"All right. All right. Geesh. You millennials are such wimps."

Millennials? Sam ignored him and made his way to the side door. He peered through the window at an empty kitchen. Slowly he turned the handle while keeping his rifle raised. The door cracked open, barely letting out a groan. "I'm going in," he said to Carl over the radio. "You still got eyes on them?"

"Oh you're fine. These losers are having a whale of a time."

He didn't elaborate on what that meant but the lack of urgency in his voice didn't quite go with the situation. Sam pushed into the dark home; candle flames caused his shadow to dance on the walls as he moved forward ready to engage. He scanned the kitchen. It was in a mess, unwashed dishes all over the countertops, fly-ridden food spilling out of a garbage can. The smell was atrocious like someone had defecated. He pressed on until he heard voices. Two males, hooting and hollering.

"I told you we shouldn't have done that last house. It was a close call."

"Close but at least we got this, right?"

"Yeah but…"

The guy's voice cut off as Sam's foot pressed down on a piece of loose floorboard and it creaked. Sam backed up quickly, slipping into the closest room to him. It was a small bedroom, a girl's room. Clothes were scattered all over the floor and single bed. Posters of bands had been torn and the walls had been graffitied with lewd words.

"Anything?" a guy's voice said from just beyond the door.

"Nah, must have been the wind."

Sam got on the radio to get confirmation that the guy had returned. "What about the one upstairs?"

"Still there."

He didn't waste any time, he stepped back out into the corridor and moved towards the living room with his back pressed against the wall. As he came into the living room that was illuminated with candles, he noticed the two guys had their backs turned.

"Police. Don't move." Both of them froze. "Keep your hands where I can see them. There are snipers outside with your heads in their crosshairs, just waiting for the word. Don't give them a reason." He approached them and told them to turn. As they turned, he noticed they weren't armed, and they sure as hell didn't look like they were a threat. One was around nineteen, he had a thick head of hair but looked scrawny. The other couldn't have been more than thirteen, ginger hair, lots of freckles and chubby. On a table in front of them were cans of tuna that were open. Candy wrappers everywhere, chips, and opened lemonade.

"Look, we didn't mean to hurt her. She came at us with a knife, I had no choice but to defend myself," the older one of the guys said. "We're just really hungry."

"And the three women?"

"What women?"

Sam reeled off their names and addresses. They looked at each other confused. "We haven't touched any women. That house tonight was the first one we hit. I didn't want to do it but we've run out of supplies and I didn't think anyone was home. Then that owner woke up and well, the rest is history. Sorry about striking you but…" he trailed off going white in the face.

Sam scanned the table and then got back on the radio. "Come on in," he said to Carl. He turned back to the teens. "Who are you and where is Jenn?"

"Upstairs."

Sam called out to her and he heard footsteps coming down the staircase. "What is going on?"

"You know these boys?"

"Yeah, they're my nephews. Brian and Keith."

"And all that food?"

She looked at them and the table. "They said they

found it. Brian?"

"Sorry. I…"

"Oh man," Jenn said.

"We were hungry."

Sam groaned and lowered his rifle. He couldn't believe this. He told them to wait there while he stepped out. Carl was entering as he headed down the corridor.

"Wrong people?"

"Right people, wrong crime. They broke into that lady's house to get food, not to hurt her."

Carl smirked. "And you believe them?"

"I believe Jenn, besides, whoever is behind the death of that woman in the park, they wouldn't be sitting on their ass with their hands in the air. As for the look on their faces, it was like catching a kid with his hand in the cookie jar." He ran a hand over his face just as Tom stepped in.

"You got them?"

"In the bag," Sam said.

Tom charged forward as if he was about to do

something stupid. Sam put up a hand. "Now Tom, just back up."

"Back up? Back up. And what? Let you guys throw them in a cell?"

"Actually that's for the judge to decide, and there appears to have been a little bit of a mix-up."

"No mix-up," Tom replied. "Those assholes…"

Sam placed a hand on his shoulder and led him out. "Let us take care of it from here, Tom. Okay. Trust me. They aren't going to get away with what they've done, but right now having you blow your top isn't going to help matters. Understand?"

"I understand that you cops don't know shit about justice."

With that said he trudged off.

"Tom. Wait up. We'll give you a lift home."

He turned and flashed the middle finger. "I'll walk."

Sam ran a tired hand over his face. He needed to speak with Teresa McKenna, Castine's town manager, and see if he could arrange to get more bodies in uniforms and find out what happened to the two that had volunteered. There was only so much they could do between them. He wanted to go around to each of the homes, talk to people, see if anyone else had seen or heard anything. Three women didn't just disappear without someone noticing something. One was dead, but where were the other two?

Carl sidled up beside Sam and jabbed the air as he went to walk back inside. "I told you he was a character." He laughed then paused for a second. "But in all seriousness, Sam. If they're not responsible for the three missing women. That means whoever is, is still out there."

Chapter 12

The way she saw it, that girl had done her a favor. Willow had got a little too big for her britches; and anyway, Lilith didn't like sharing Bosley with her. It was interfering with her plans. Of course she couldn't say that out loud, girls had been killed for less. She braced herself before entering the bar. Ruby had informed her that Bosley wanted to speak with her. Speaking to him was the last thing she wanted to do, that's why she'd sent Ruby into Mountain City to deliver the oh so tragic news of Willow's demise. At least if he lashed out, Ruby would get the worst of it, not her. Strangely Ruby had returned without a scratch but informed her more were dead. It burned her to think that she couldn't have got a girl like that to work for her. That's what they needed, someone with some grit.

Lilith took a deep breath and lifted her nose.

Confidence, it was all about how she presented herself.

The smell of booze filled her nostrils and heavy music attacked her senses as she entered a room full of sweaty bikers. If she had her way, she would kill the lot of them but there were far more of them than her tiny group.

The Remington bar had been a dingy hole in the wall as far back as she could remember. It suited him and his rabble to a tee. Small round tables, peanut shells on the floor, one section of the bar charred from where someone had set it on fire accidentally. A few neon signs, and dim lights powered by two solar generators out back. Around the walls were booths with black leather seating that had seen better days. Since the Reapers had rolled into town, it looked even worse.

She stepped over a broken stool and someone who was out cold. Dead? Drunk? Hard eyes bore into her as she made her way to the back of the room. She hated coming here, that's why she stayed in Neva. It was home. She knew it well and it beat spending her time waiting hand and foot on Bosley. Of course coming up with a good reason why had been essential. She said they could prevent trouble entering the town from the south. Bosley was against the idea at first until she proved herself. And she did, preventing a number of troublemakers until now.

She spotted Bosley seated at a booth with two scantily clad women either side of him. It sickened her. He'd intrigued her at first. There was an air of mystery to him. Any man who had the balls to roll into a town and take it over had to be admired or feared. But that was then. She should have figured he was just like the rest of them — an egotistical womanizer.

"Lilith." He slapped the two girls on the legs and gestured for them to leave. They slipped out, glancing at her. "Come. Take a seat. We need to talk."

"I'll stand."

"That wasn't a question." He gave a nod and she slipped in across from him.

The table in front of her was covered in white powder, empty bottles of beer and glasses. There was a plate of nachos and meat in front of him. He reached for one and stuffed it into his mouth. He stared at her as he chewed and she could feel his eyes burning holes through her. He cleared his palate with a swig of beer and leaned back with his arms spread across the back of the leather. "You want to tell me how it happened?"

"I thought Ruby had."

"You mean, you hoped Ruby had." He snorted. "What? You think sending her here would somehow get you off the hook?"

"It wasn't my fault."

He exploded forward, his hand smashing the table. "Don't do that. Don't shift the blame. You were put in charge of those women. You told me you could handle it. Now how many are dead?"

"Several."

"Several," he repeated. "And this girl. Who is she?"

"I don't know. She was with a guy. He said he was traveling to Castine, Maine."

"And this guy? Where is he?"

"I…"

He slammed his fist down again.

ALL THAT SURVIVES: A Post-Apocalyptic EMP Survival Thriller

Her eyes widened. "All I know is that they were heading this way. Surely some of your men saw them enter?"

"My men?"

"Or have they been too busy getting liquored up?"

He jabbed his finger at her. "Careful! Careful what you say next."

"Or what? You gonna slit my throat like you did those other girls? Or hang me like the residents of this town?" She leaned forward. "The reason you aren't in the ground right now is because of me. So... two people slipped through my fingers but have you forgotten all of those who didn't? Those state police officers? That group of hunters? If it wasn't for us, a lot more of your men would be dead." She leaned back, her frown relaxing.

He sneered. "I want this girl."

"As do I but it looks like we are in the same boat because she's vanished."

"You lost her?"

"You know how big those woods are?"

"Whatever," he said reaching for his beer.

"Why haven't you got your men looking for them?"

"Because we have you for that."

She chuckled.

"What's so funny?" he asked.

"You and I are very much alike. Maybe that's why I fell for your bullshit when you rolled into town. Now you make me sick."

He lit a cigarette and blew smoke in her direction "You don't like this arrangement?" He raised an eyebrow. "Huh?"

When she didn't answer he slipped around the table, then grabbed her by the neck. "You might have gained a following but don't forget who's running the show. Are we clear?" He squeezed the back of her neck tighter. "Are we clear?"

She shrugged him off. "Crystal."

"Before the night is over, I want this bitch found, and the guy. They can't have got far."

She slipped out of the booth. "And Lilith."

She looked back at him without responding.

"You ever let this happen again and you know what I will do."

He didn't need to explain, the smell coming from the dumpster outside sent a clear message to those who knew him. His patience was thin, his loyalty only as deep as the loyalty given. She exited the bar cursing under her breath. His day was coming even if it meant slitting his throat in bed. Outside several women waited for her. She yelled at them. "Get out there. Go find this girl. Find out what people have seen."

Mountain City was in the middle of nowhere, surrounded by mountains and forest. Anyone on foot wouldn't get far and while Bosley looked as if he was doing nothing, looks could be deceiving. Scattered throughout the town were his men, positioned on rooftops, behind windows and among the families of the few remaining residents. The town of two thousand had been reduced considerably after the blackout. He'd simply taken it down a few more notches.

If they were still nearby it was only a matter of time before someone turned them in.

* * *

"I still don't understand why you've been holed up in here for the past two days?" Landon asked. "Why not just walk out of here?"

"Because they'll see you."

"Who?"

"Reapers. Man, have you not been listening to anything I've said?" Robbie scoffed.

"I didn't see anyone out there. The town is deserted barring those guys over at that bar."

"That's what they want you to think." He bit into an apple. "They're out there. How you managed to get this far without being spotted is truly remarkable."

"We came in via the south end."

"Well that kind of explains things. The bulk of Bosley's men are dispersed throughout the rest of the town. The south end is handled by Lilith and crew. Not many slip by her, that's for sure. Bitch is a nutcase."

"You know her?"

"Of course." He chuckled. He finished his apple and tossed it into the garbage. He was a strange man and Landon had a sense he was holding back information. He still wasn't sure what to call him, Robbie or his odd rap name.

Robbie reached into his pocket for a cigarette, slapping his lips as if satisfied with what Landon had fed him. He'd come to learn that he'd actually been eating dog food for the past two days. Yep, straight out of the can. That's what came from holing up inside an animal clinic. "So tell me more about this town of yours. What's it like out that way? I've heard it's nice. I always wanted to go east to the shore and see the whales."

Landon looked back out the window. He'd been trying to figure out the best time to head out because bikes kept roaring by. "Look, Robbie, I would love to sit here and have this conversation but I still have a long way to go before I reach Damascus."

"So you're gonna wait for her."

Landon stole a glance over his shoulder and frowned. "I don't know if she's coming back. She left a long time ago. I appreciate all she did but I have to keep moving. My family is out there and…"

"They're all you've got," Robbie said.

Landon nodded. "What about you? You got family?"

He returned to looking out.

"Yeah."

"Where are they?"

Robbie got up off the floor. "Look, I'll come with you."

"No. I travel alone."

"You weren't traveling alone."

"Robbie. No offense but I don't know you. You don't know me. Besides, didn't you say you had family?' He was still waiting for a response but Robbie seemed a little reluctant to talk about it. Either they were dead or he was ashamed of them.

"Look, I can get you out of here."

"Really? That's why you've been hiding in here? Nice

try but…"

"I know how this town works. I know where his men are."

"Then why haven't you left?"

His chin dropped. "There's a girl."

Landon rocked his head back and nodded, a smile forming. "Isn't there always," he replied.

"I can't leave without her."

"This girl of yours got a name?"

"Shelby. She's uh…" Robbie inhaled deeply.

"How long you known her?"

"As long as we've…" He went to say something but stopped and looked at Landon. "Look, it doesn't matter. All that matters is that I know how to get out of this town without being spotted, but I'm not going without her and if I was you, I would at least wait. Give this girl… Beth a little more time. Sounds like she went out of her way to help you. It's the least you can do."

Uh, that was all he needed. A guilt trip. It wasn't that he wanted to leave her behind but he didn't know if she'd return. The odds were stacked against her and common sense told him that she was probably... he squeezed his eyes shut not wanting to think about what they were doing to her if they had her.

"Okay, look. Let's say I stick around and help you get this girl of yours. How do we get out of here? Where are his men?"

"You got a map?"

"Not of this town."

"All right," Robbie said, looking around the room. He started taking things down from the shelves and laying them out on the ground. He then took some kibble and started dropping it down in a line.

"Robbie, what the hell are you doing?"

"Laying out the town. Shit. What's it look like?"

Landon raised his eyebrows and looked out the window, letting him get on with it. Under the cover of darkness it was hard to see much except for silhouettes of people moving along the street. He assumed that was Bosley's men or Lilith's people trying to find them.

"All right. Here we go," he said. "Come. Take a look."

Landon turned and Robbie was holding a long metal stick in his hand. "Okay, we are here. Bosley's men are positioned. Here, here, here, here, here, here and here." He took a breath and continued pointing out even more areas. "There are two guys on this building. One is situated here. Now if we move down this street here, between the times of eight and ten, no one will be looking because they change shift and—"

"Hold on a second. How do you know all of this?"

"I told you. I know this town like the back of my hand."

Landon raised a hand. "Yeah, but aren't these areas only known to them?'

Robbie screwed up his face.

"What are you not telling me, Robbie?"

He cleared his throat and kicked the ground a little.

"Robbie."

"Okay. I admit it. I'm one of them."

"You didn't kill for that jacket?"

"Oh no, I did. I mean, to earn the patch but the guy wasn't a Reaper, so no."

Landon swallowed hard and his hand slipped down to his handgun.

"Hey. Hey. I might have been one of them but I'm not anymore."

"How do I know that?" Landon asked.

"Because I wouldn't be in here."

"How do I know that this isn't your lookout spot?"

"Uh… because…" He charged over to a couple of empty cans. "Would I eat dog food if everything was good between me and them?" He tossed a can on the ground.

"Who knows? You're a little weird."

"Weird?"

"The whole Denzel rap shit."

"What, because I'm white and in a biker gang, I can't rap?"

"So now you're in a biker gang?"

"No. Now you're putting words in my mouth."

"Robbie. Explain before I…"

He put his hands up and backed up. "Okay. How do I explain this?" He paced back and forth.

"Maybe start at the beginning."

He groaned and ran a hand around the back of his neck. "The girl. Shelby. You know, I've not had much luck with women, Landon. When I met her I thought things would be different. We got on really well but then Bosley. He had to go screw it up. Couldn't let me have a good thing. Oh no, he's got the pick of any girl he wants and yet he wants mine."

"So you bumped heads with him."

"Something like that." He nodded.

"Why didn't you just take her?"

"Because he stopped me. What was I meant to do."

"Kill him?"

Robbie looked back at him. "Kill my own brother?"

Chapter 13

It was the perfect cover. Gareth had an agreement with the Reapers to deliver wild game to them. He was one of a handful of hunters that were allowed to live in exchange for their services. There was no set schedule as to when he had to drop it off, only that it had to be done once a week. When Beth asked why he did what they wanted, Gareth said it was better to deal with the devil you know than the devil you don't. "The country has become a very bleak place to live. Run? Yes. I could do that. But how long would I last out there before someone puts a bullet in the back of my head? At least here I can stay in my own hometown, sandwiched between Lilith and Bosley, and close to those I know," he said looking at the pastor. "And while the Reapers are assholes, they go to great lengths to protect their investment. That's what I am to them. An investment." He tossed another dead animal in the back of his truck and pulled back the tarp. "Go on,

ALL THAT SURVIVES: A Post-Apocalyptic EMP Survival Thriller

get in."

Pastor Michaels gave Beth a hand lifting Grizzly into the back. The elk and sheep were already gutted, and chopped into pieces, though there were a few animals that were still in there that hadn't been touched.

Unconvinced by his answer, Beth peppered him with more questions. He answered saying that he didn't see it as a major inconvenience, he already had to catch his own food, collecting a few more animals didn't matter to him. Besides, the kickback of free moonshine was a strong incentive. When he walked away, Pastor Michaels told her that was his only weakness or downfall.

"Are you sure I can trust him?" Beth asked the pastor as she slipped under a tarp in the back of the Chevy truck while Gareth collected his rifle from inside the trailer.

Had she not been around animal carcasses all her life she might have had trouble crawling in there with Grizzly but it was either that or hike it and she'd already been gone long enough. She had started to wonder if Landon would stick around.

"He's fine. A few screws loose but he's a good friend and I trust him."

She raised an eyebrow and the pastor squeezed her hand. "You'll be fine. Just do as he says and by this time tomorrow this will just be a bad memory."

"I hope," she replied. She cozied up with the dead animals and pulled the thick blue tarp over the two of them. It crumpled in her grasp. Grizzly sniffed at a deer and began to chew on a limb. "You hungry, boy?" She took out a knife and carved a few pieces of flesh off the bone. Grizzly guzzled them down waiting for more. She didn't think Gareth would mind. At least one of them wouldn't go hungry.

The trailer door slammed shut and she heard the pastor giving him strict instructions. Gareth replied, "Yeah, yeah. It's all good."

"Take care, Beth," the pastor said patting the side of the truck. She replied, thanking him before the suspension dipped as Gareth got in and started the engine. It would be a short fifteen-minute drive.

The motion of the truck nearly lulled her into a sleep. Beth leaned back only to have the truck bounce over uneven ground and she caught air. She groaned as her shoulder slammed into the metal. She kept a tight grip on Grizzly and a strap that held the tarp down. The flesh stank. She lifted her top over her lower face and peered out the rear watching the silhouette of Neva disappear. She couldn't help but feel relieved to be leaving it behind.

"Not long now, boy," she said.

Gareth had told her to stay low and not look out. Once he made it into Mountain City he would park near the bar and let them know he'd brought the goods, at which point he would distract them by leading them into the bar and she could slip out. From there she was on her own. It seemed straightforward enough.

As they got closer, she heard motorbikes roaring by. Curious to see, she peeked out and saw some of the women veering off down a street as they made their way into Mountain City.

The truck started to slow and she heard voices, male,

deep.

"About time."

"I'm feeling a cookout coming on."

"Hey boys!" Gareth yelled as he veered the truck outside the bar. She peered out and saw lots of motorbikes angled to one side and six gruff-looking biker dudes in leather lingering outside, all were heavily armed.

The engine shut off and boots approached.

"Another batch?"

"Why, you getting too many?" Gareth asked.

A biker chuckled. "Never."

"That's what I thought."

Beth heard him hop out and one of the men got close and went to lift the tarp. "Hey, don't spoil the merchandise," Gareth said slapping down the tarp. She felt a shot of fear go through her at the thought of being caught. Grizzly went to adjust his position and she had to force him down. She mouthed the word *wait* as if he could read lips. "Bosley around?"

"Inside."

ALL THAT SURVIVES: A Post-Apocalyptic EMP Survival Thriller

"How about we all get some drinks?" Gareth said.

She heard them walk away and a door opened. Music strained out and then it went quiet. Moving ever so slowly, Beth glanced out. There was no one outside. "Okay, let's go," she said lifting the tarp and motioning for Grizzly to jump out. He bounced over the tailgate and she dropped down and whistled to him as she scanned the area. Good, no one was around. Right then as Beth turned to head around the building, a guy came into view zipping up his jeans. He glanced up and Beth got this oh shit look on her face as he went for his handgun. Before she could get an arrow on the bow, Grizzly leapt on the man taking him down.

"Grizzly." She hurried over, bow in hand and fired an arrow into the guy's chest before he could harm the dog. No sooner had she done that than the door to the bar opened and two bikers staggered out. They glanced her way, their eyes dropped to their fallen comrade and all hell broke loose. She managed to get one arrow off before coming under the hail of gunfire.

Beth blasted away from the bar, Grizzly bounding beside her as yelling ensued. Her eyes darted from side to side, she turned and fired another arrow, that one missed. She was down to three as they hurried across Old South Church Road and cut through a yard behind a house. The trouble with properties in the vicinity was they weren't closed off with fences, it was all open space which meant losing them wouldn't be easy. Slinging her bow over her shoulder, she pulled the rifle, dropped and squeezed off three rounds. One struck a biker in the upper thigh, buckling his legs.

By now there had to be eight, maybe more on her trail. She stared in horror as more streamed around the side of the bar, yelling, some jumping on motorcycles. Her stomach tightened. The guttural roar of an engine ignited her adrenaline and her legs pounded the ground trying to escape.

If she was caught, it was all over.

Somewhere amid the twists and turns around trees and homes she became disoriented. Was she heading back or away from the bar? Everything was beginning to look the same. Where was the area she'd left Landon? Headlights flashed, illuminating the night. Guns erupted.

All she knew was to keep running.

She yelled at Grizzly to keep him from being distracted from those in pursuit.

They darted between an auto shop and a home, down a back alley, across a field, through a junkyard and scrambled over the top of mounds of soil that a construction company had piled up nearby. Casting a fearful glance over her shoulder she nearly ran into a biker who had cut off her escape. He opened fire and dropped behind a dumpster then hurried back the other way. "Grizzly. Come on!" she yelled; her mind overwhelmed, anguish rising and getting the better of her. She could feel tears welling in her eyes at the thought of what they'd do if they caught her. Killing Willow was one thing, killing some of their own…

If it hadn't been dark, she was sure they would have found her by now.

Darting in and out of alleys, staying low behind buildings, vehicles and garbage cans, anything that could hide her, she managed to make it into a car lot that had a few stalled vehicles, some had been torn apart. As she backed up, keeping her gaze on four bikers who were shining flashlights nearby, she suddenly felt a hand wrap around her mouth and yank her backward. Her breath caught in her throat and she reacted defensively, spinning and lashing out only to strike Landon in the face. "Landon?!"

"What the hell," he said rubbing his jaw.

She helped him up and a stranger appeared from an open door and beckoned them in. Grizzly shot in first, followed by her and Landon, then the door was shut and they were swallowed by darkness.

"Don't move. Don't make a sound," the stranger said.

They remained silent, crouched on the ground. Beyond the door they could hear yelling, bikers making guesses on which way she'd gone.

"This way."

"No. Over here."

"I'm sure I saw her dart into that home."

Eventually the noise faded and she looked at Landon and he smiled pulling her in for a hug. It was kind of odd. She wasn't his daughter but over the course of four months they'd formed a bond that felt special. That all faded when he opened his mouth. "I'm glad you made it. I nearly left without you."

Her brow furrowed. "What?"

"I didn't think you were coming back… or that you'd even make it back."

"So you were just gonna leave me here?"

Landon got up. "I told you not to go."

"Yeah. And leave Grizzly behind." She shook her head. "I should have stayed in North Carolina." She got up and looked at the stranger. "And who the hell is this?"

Enthusiastically he extended his hand. "Robbie Holmes but most call me Denzel."

She frowned and Landon shook his head. "It's a long story. Don't even ask."

They wandered to the front of the clinic. Landon was full of questions.

"How did you make it back?"

"You don't even want to know," she said wiping sweat from her brow. She took off her jacket because she was overheating. "You got a drink?" she asked.

"Yeah, one sec." Robbie hurried over to a bag and returned with some water. Landon looked over and then realized he'd taken it out of his bag. Beth finished what was left of it, wiped her lips with the back of her arm and looked around.

"Lucky you spotted me otherwise I would have been out there searching for you."

"Like I said, I didn't know you were coming back."

"But you were just gonna leave me?"

"I…"

"Don't you ever do that," she said, stabbing her finger at him. The memory of her father came back to her and reopened the wound of grief. She looked down and saw pet food all over the ground and different cans stacked up. "What the hell is that?" she asked.

Seeing his opportunity to impress, Robbie bounced on the balls of his feet and hurried over, taking her through his model of the town. "And this is where we can escape."

"Then let's go," she said tossing the Platypus bag back to Landon. She went to walk by him and he pulled her back.

"Slow down. You wanna die?"

"No. But they'll be checking everywhere."

Landon placed a hand on her again. "Robbie. Tell her where they're located," Landon said, shaking his head as he crossed the room to the window. He pulled away and watched as Robbie used the makeshift town on the floor to point out every building, alley, and home that had bikers.

"So we're in the maze from hell," she replied.

"That about sums it up," Robbie said.

As she walked around the room, she noticed Robbie was looking her up and down. "Take a picture, it might last longer," she said.

He grinned. "Landon never said how good you look."

"What?" she replied, her cheeks going slightly flushed.

"Robbie, manners," Landon said before looking back out the window.

"Why are you wearing one of their jackets?"

Robbie's eyes bounced between her and Landon. Landon spoke up, "Bosley is his brother."

Her eyes widened. "You're his brother?" she said slowly, almost with a tone of disgust.

"He's fine. Trust me. If he wasn't, he'd be dead by now," Landon said.

Beth raised a finger. "Robbie, you mind if I have a word with Landon?"

"Go ahead."

"In private."

"Oh. Right. Sure. I'll step out back," he replied turning to head out. As he walked past Grizzly, the dog growled at him when he went to pat him. Robbie pulled back his hand and looked at Beth. "I'm sure he'll warm up to me later."

She waited until he was out of the room before she asked, "You trust this guy?"

"That guy saved me. Well, possibly," Landon replied, a look of confusion on his face.

She scowled. "But he's one of them."

"Actually I'm not," Robbie replied from out back.

"I thought I said… privately," Beth said.

"Kind of hard. It's a small building. I can hear you."

She shook her head and shifted her weight from one foot to the next. "Okay, so you have the layout of the town and you trust him to get us out, but when is that meant to happen?"

"Tonight," Robbie said stepping back into the room.

"Robbie. It's crazy out there," Landon said.

"It's the one time that the bar won't have all of these guys inside. Shelby's in there. I'm going in. Tonight. And if you want to get out then I'm going to need your help."

Beth shook her finger in the air and stepped between them. "Anyone care to explain who Shelby is?"

"Just a goddess," Robbie said.

"Of course." She shook her head and crossed the room and took a seat to calm her nerves. Her heart was still thumping in her chest. She looked up at Landon. "Didn't think it was going to be this hard, did you?"

"No."

"And you still want to go to Maine?"

"Want doesn't come into it. I need to."

She placed her hands on her knees and dropped her head. "This is going to be the death of me but all right. How do we help you?" she asked Robbie.

Chapter 14

Beth was skeptical but that all changed when Robbie shared his plan. Now she was worried. Robbie's hatred for the gang ran far deeper than his brother stealing his girl out from under his nose. "You want to do what?" she asked.

"If you think we're going to waltz in there and scoop her out without a distraction, you are mistaken. I know what my brother values. We hit him where it hurts. He'll respond. He already knows I'm here. And with you two on the loose he will have no choice but to handle this himself."

"But it's your brother."

"He stopped being that a long time ago."

They'd gone back and forth on what was the best approach to get Shelby but with only Robbie knowing how his brother would coordinate the bikers, they had to trust him. Still, that didn't stop Beth from trying to talk

Landon out of it.

While Robbie prepared for their departure to the first stop, she pulled Landon aside. "I don't like this."

"He gave you the chance to provide an alternative. It makes sense what he wants to do. It's risky but so is trying to navigate it out of the town. We won't make it two streets before they come after us. So I say we follow his lead. See if there is any weight to his idea and give it a shot."

She exhaled hard, exasperated, glancing at Robbie.

Who was this man? How did he wind up being a part of this biker group? Everyone had a story and she was sure she'd learn his in time if they survived the night.

"All right. You ready?" Robbie asked.

They nodded.

"Beth. Your dog. You might be better off leaving him here until we get back."

"Grizzly comes with me."

Robbie's gaze bounced to Landon but he shrugged. "Don't look at me. I've already been through this with her." With that said Robbie looked out the window one final time before unlocking the door at the rear of the clinic and they rolled out.

The Exxon gas station was located two blocks away.

They moved in a line, keeping their backs to the wall. While Beth was confident that Grizzly would stay close, she couldn't risk it and had leashed him to her waist using a leash from the clinic. She kept a firm grip as they charged forward down Main Street, using the buildings around them as cover. From one structure to the next they darted in and out of the shadows. Every now and again Robbie threw up a hand and they dropped and waited for a passing bike or truck to roll by.

Beside the gas station was a two-story real estate office that had been broken into, they ducked into there and climbed the steps to the exit that led out to the roof so they could get a better lay of the land. Beth didn't think it was a good idea to have them all at street level as there were too many of Bosley's men and Lilith's sluts searching for them.

There was an alleyway that ran between the real estate office and a NAPA Auto Parts store that butted up against the gas station. "So how do you want to do this?" Beth asked. Robbie had been tight lipped about the logistics of how he wanted to go about it, only saying where he wanted to go. Within seconds of answering, she realized why.

"We'll jump over to the NAPA building. Once on top of there, we can climb directly onto the gas station."

"You want to run that by me again? We or you?" Landon said. "Just a reminder I have a leg that is still healing."

"Okay, Beth and I will do it. You stay here and look after Grizzly."

Beth shook her head. "Alright. I'm out. This is insane." She stabbed her finger at Landon, and pointed at Robbie. "This is why I said we should part ways."

"You did?" Robbie asked. "But I thought we had a thing."

"A thing?" Beth asked.

"Yeah, you know."

She stared at him. "Are you joking? You think we have a thing from a creepy eye stare?"

"I thought we were on the same frequency."

Beth ran a hand over her weary face and approached him. "This girl of yours. She know about this? You think she would mind you having... a thing with another girl?" She rolled her eyes.

"We are open minded to relationships."

"Really? Well obviously, it's too open as your brain has dropped out." She turned to walk back to the door that led into the real estate office. "Let's go, Grizzly." The dog followed without hesitation.

"Beth. Beth!" Landon said, raising a hand to Robbie as if to indicate he wanted a word with her. He crossed the short distance between them and pursed his lips and pointed to the edge of the building, leading her away from Robbie. "Look, I know he's strange."

"Strange? More like fucking insane. I mean, seriously. What are we doing here, Landon? You want to get home?

Home is out there. Not here."

His brow furrowed. "Don't you think I know that?" He paused to catch his breath. "But if he's right, then the odds of us getting out of this town are slim to none. Think about it."

"Oh I've thought about it," she said. "And I think he's stringing us along. This is all some game. Seriously. Are we meant to believe that someone who has holed up inside an animal clinic for two days eating dog food has stuck around for some girl that he didn't have the balls to go and get, but has waited until we came along? C'mon! No, something is fishy about this. About him. About this town. And I say we get out now before we can't."

"You don't want to jump. I'll do it."

"What? You can't do it. You said so yourself a minute ago."

"That was before you decided to leave."

He turned and walked back to Robbie. Beth stood there looking at him. Landon looked back at her while he talked with him. "Damn it," she muttered under her breath. Why had she agreed to this? She crossed over to him and put up a hand. "Once this is over, we go our separate ways."

"Who, you and me?" Landon asked.

"No. Us and him." She turned to Robbie who was looking sheepish. For a man that was supposed to run with a badass biker gang, he certainly gave off a wimpish vibe. "So… we doing this or what?" She turned to Grizzly and told him to wait with Landon then crossed over to the edge and looked down. It was hard to gauge distance accurately at night. Of course they could make out the silhouette of the rooftop they were about to jump onto, but from the real estate roof it looked too wide.

"Looks impossible to me," she said.

"You're just saying that because you want us to leave."

"I'm not saying leave, but we can go down and around."

"The fact that we haven't got spotted until now is a surprise. But that place has the gasoline we need." He nodded. "Yeah. It was one of the first buildings that my brother secured. The pumps aren't working but siphoning gas up from the tanks below ground, that was doable."

"Okay, maybe three months ago. But gasoline has a shelf life of three to six months. It degrades."

"You're right. But we're only four months in and we aren't using it to power a generator or fuel a vehicle, which I might add still works. So whoever taught you that lesson about shelf life needs to brush up," he said in a smug way before looking back over the lip of the roof. "Besides, even if we went down, they'd see us. There are four guys inside. And they are not coming out. They never come out except to change shifts. They protect that gas with their life."

Robbie rolled his shoulders around, limbered up and crossed to the opposite side of the building with Beth watching from the edge. She had to see this. She fully expected him to miss and go knees first into the edge of the building or land on his face. "Well let's get this shit on the road," he said rolling his head around. He slapped himself a few times in the face like a mental patient, probably to build courage to jump, then he dropped down like a runner at the starting line. "Here goes nothing."

His legs exploded as he sprinted towards the lip of the roof and hopped up onto the edge and launched himself off. Beth watched in awe as he soared over the gap and landed hard on the gravel surface of the NAPA roof, going straight into a roll. He got up and dusted himself off and looked at her with a smile. "A walk in the park."

She pursed her lips and mumbled under her breath. "A walk in the park. I'll give him a walk in the park," she said as she glared at Landon. He simply shrugged, keeping a firm grip on Grizzly's leash. Grizzly barked once and both of them put a finger up to their lips.

Beth gave herself a mental pep talk. "Okay, you can do this. You've jumped farther. No you haven't," she said. "Oh shit," she said bursting forward and running towards the edge as fast as she could. The closer she got, the more her fear overwhelmed her. *No. No. I can't.* She stopped just short of the edge and felt a full panic attack coming on. She looked at Robbie and he lifted both hands, making a gesture as if to say… what are you playing at? That infuriated her. She stormed back to the far side of the building and prepared to give it another shot. Again, she pumped herself up. *You got this. You've got this.* Boom. Her foot stomped the roof as her thighs pounded like pistons. Those were the words that went through her mind as she stopped again. "Damn it!" she said in a low voice. "Forget it," she said to Robbie who didn't hear her. She dropped to a crouch and tried to catch her breath.

As she knelt there, Landon appeared at her side and placed a hand on her shoulder. He never said anything, if he had she might have been inclined to slap his hand away. Not because she was angry at him but because she was frustrated with herself. Drop her in the wilderness and she could survive with very little, but heights... That was something else. She looked up at him.

"It's the height."

"Ah," he said nodding but not adding anything to it. She felt stupid saying it. Now he knew why she wanted to go down. Among all the fears she had to conquer, was her fear of height. The fear of falling. Having no one there to catch her. Both physically and emotionally. Maybe that's why she'd been nervous to leave with Landon. Her homestead had been her security net. The one place where she felt safe. Being hidden away in the Pisgah Forest may have felt uncomfortable to others but to her it was the complete opposite.

"I just…" she trailed off and ran a hand over her face.

Landon crouched down and squeezed her shoulder. "It's okay to be scared."

"I'm not," she shot back, an instinct of self-preservation.

He tipped his head and raised an eyebrow.

She sighed and looked at Grizzly.

"What would your father say?"

She snorted. "That's not fair."

"Hey. You said he pushed you. Must have had a reason." He stared intently at her. "Look, do or don't, it doesn't matter to me. We'll head out."

"What? But what about all that stuff you said before…"

He shrugged. "Look. You aren't going to do it and I only agreed to get you to do it. But if you're too scared then that's fine." She narrowed her eyes, got up and brushed herself off again and crossed the roof. "Beth."

She looked back at him without saying anything. Made an o with her mouth and began breathing hard and then burst forward. She set her face like a flint and listened to that deep inner voice of her father, the one that always told her she could do anything any guy could. Her foot touched the lip of the roof and boosted her into the air. Like a rocket, she flew over the dark gap not looking down for even a second.

Beth landed with a thump, going straight into a roll that ended near Robbie's feet. A hand extended down. "Welcome to the other side of fear," he said. "Feels good, doesn't it?" She gripped it and he pulled her up. Beth looked back at Landon and he gave her a thumbs-up.

"Now what?" she asked.

He motioned for her to follow. He climbed up onto the gas station roof and they made their way over to the fire escape door which had a large chain and bolt on it. He asked for her hatchet. "Stand back."

He struck it hard multiple times until the chain broke away from the lock. Robbie smiled as he handed the hatchet back to her. He opened the door that led down into the guts of the station. The stairwell was a dingy space no wider than four feet that smelled of oil and grease. Some of the tiles were warped from water damage. Robbie gestured for her to go in first. He closed the door behind them and they were instantly shrouded in darkness. Slowly she descended the metal steps until she could hear voices and rock music.

At the bottom of the stairwell, Beth inched up to a door and slowly eased it open to get a better look at what they were dealing with. Inside were four men playing cards around a table. A couple of AR-15's were leaning up against their chairs as they sat there shooting the breeze and tossing out a few cards to one another. One was smoking a large cigar and blowing clouds of gray smoke at the face of one of his pals who was swatting it away in an annoyed fashion. The other two were knocking back beer from cans with one of them counting coins in front of him.

"Come on. Play your cards. What you got?"

Beth looked at Robbie. "Where's the gas and oil kept?"

He pointed to an area beyond the men.

She shook her head. "We're not getting past them."

He pulled out a revolver and tapped it against the side of his temple like some kind of psycho. "Where there is a will there is a way." As she turned, Robbie's arm wrapped around her throat and yanked her back before he grabbed the door and swung it open.

"Hey boys! Look what I found!"

Chapter 15

"What the hell are you playing at?!" she muttered but Robbie didn't reply. Shock gripped her. Was this some kind of game? He was keeping his arm tight around her neck. She could have got out of it if she wanted to but it happened so fast that the four men were up and had rifles in their hands.

A troll of a man with dark hair and goatee frowned. "Robbie? Where the hell did you come from?" Quick on his feet, he made up some bogus story about coming through the rear exit and finding her lurking outside. He then reprimanded them for leaving the door open. Whatever hope she had of this being some kind of ambush evaporated when Robbie shoved her forward right into the midst of them. "Next time you need to be more careful. That bitch could have shot all of you."

A beefy bald guy clasped onto the back of her and pressed his nose into her hair. "Like sweet cherry pie. I get first dibs on her."

Beth reacted by elbowing him in the gut and trying to make a break for it only to be slammed in the side of the face with the butt of a gun. Her body slumped over a table and the bald guy cursed, grabbing hold of her again. "Oh you like it rough, do you?"

"Hey," Robbie said. "Now you want to tell me what you knuckleheads are doing playing cards? Aren't you meant to be making sure no one waltzes in here and steals the gas?"

"We were just having a little fun. Shit. We've been in here for hours. Besides, I heard your brother was looking for you. Said something about you killing Carson. That true?"

"If it was, do you think I would still be here?" Robbie strolled over to the table and snatched up a beer belonging to one of them and downed it in front of them. Not one of them stopped him. Held down over the table, she watched it play out while the bald guy kept his hand on her back. "Did you fellas not get the memo about her and another guy killing several of ours?"

"Yeah, we got the heads-up. A little after being told to keep an eye out for you."

"Me? Please. Sit your asses down. You're not spinning this around and squirming your way out of your screw-up. I have a good mind to tell Bosley and have you transferred to shit duty." Their eyes widened. Beth had no idea what that involved but with sanitation being one of the greatest problems facing the country without power, she figured they were burying it. "Yeah. I can do that," Robbie said.

"What do you want?" Goatee Guy asked.

"Those Molotov cocktails we created. Where are they?"

"Why?"

"Why?" Robbie asked. Beth noticed he'd taken on a completely different persona to the one she'd seen. Here he was strolling around like he owned the joint or was in charge of their group. "Because Bosley wants them. You want to discuss it with him?"

All four of them stared back and looked at each other. "Out back."

"Good. Keep an eye on her," he said walking out back.

Left alone, the guys looked at her. "So you're the mouse causing all the trouble. Little mouse, your night just took a turn for the worst," Baldy said leaning down and licking the side of her face. She brought her leg up and ground her foot into his shin causing him to cry out in pain and slap her. Beth hit the floor and one of them placed his foot on her as she tried to crawl away. "You aren't going anywhere, little mouse."

"Hey, one of you guys give me a hand loading these into the truck," Robbie yelled.

"I'll go," the smallest of them said exiting the room.

A few minutes passed and she had to listen to those animals talk about what they were going to do to her once Robbie was out of their hair. She tried to wriggle but Baldy just pressed his foot into her back. "I can't breathe," she said but they just ignored her. A minute, maybe two, Robbie ducked his head in from out back.

"Need an extra hand." Robbie pointed to one of them.

Troll Boy gave a nod and followed him out. *No. No. Don't go.* He was the only one that was preventing Baldy from taking advantage of her. As soon as the door slammed shut, Baldy crouched down beside her. "You're mine."

A gun went off and both of them looked towards the door.

"Ashford? Monroe? Robbie?"

There was no answer.

"You want me to go see?" the third guy asked. Baldy nodded and as he crossed the room toward the door, it opened and Robbie staggered in, gripping his stomach which looked to be covered in blood. His face was smeared red. "Lock the door. They got the other two."

"What? Who?"

"Lock the door."

Baldy released his foot and hurried for the door just as Robbie pulled his revolver out of his waistband behind his back and squeezed a round into the guy closest to her.

Baldy turned, his face registered shock before a round hit him square in the skull and he dropped. Beth looked on, her eyes wide, as Robbie glanced at her and raised his hand which was covered in blood. "It's not mine. See," he said lifting his top to show there was no blood. "Like I said… where there is a will there is a way."

She bounced up and smashed both hands into his chest knocking him back.

"You ever do that again and I will kill you myself."

"Wow, princess. That's a little harsh. I just saved your ass and got us what we needed. A little thanks is in order."

She tossed him the bird and barreled past him about to leave.

Robbie lifted a hand. "Listen, I knew if I told you what I was planning, you wouldn't have done it or it wouldn't have come across as genuine. They needed to buy it, and buy it they did," he said. "Come on, Beth."

"Man, you're an asshole."

"But a cute one, right?" He grinned.

She glared at him and he followed her out. "Look, we

have to make the molotov cocktails. They didn't do it. It won't take us long." As he led her out to a storage room she stepped over the bodies of the other guys. One had been strangled, the other shot. Robbie had taken the blood from the troll boy and wiped it on the front of his shirt. She had to give him credit, it was clever, risky but clever. He pointed to a crate of empty beer bottles. "Bring those over here." She slid them over by pushing them with her foot. She watched him go through the process of gathering together gasoline and oil, and then tearing some rag. He filled each bottle until it was around 70 percent full using two-thirds gasoline and one-third oil. "Well don't stand there. Give me a hand. The sooner we get these together, the quicker we get out of here."

Beth crouched and tore apart a sheet.

"What were you planning on doing with these?"

"What?" he asked, distracted as he poured gasoline into a funnel.

"They knew what you were referring to when you mentioned the Molotov cocktails. What was the deal?"

He chuckled and nodded. "Ah that. Yeah. When we rolled into town not long after the blackout, Bosley, my brother, had this idea to ensure people didn't fight back. I mean, we didn't know how many were still in this town. A hundred and forty of us against two thousand wouldn't have gone well. However we were fortunate. A lot of people died in those first two weeks; others left town. By the time we rolled in, there couldn't have been more than four, maybe five hundred residents."

"Still, that's a lot," she said.

"You give people too much credit. These folks aren't fighters. Most are blue-collar workers. You get the odd hunter who knows how to shoot but you gotta have balls to do that and not many do. That's why it surprises me."

"What does?" She tucked a piece of rag into the bottle and placed it down.

"You. No offense but you don't strike me as..."

"Strong?" she asked.

"Uh..." He was at a loss for words.

"No, I get it. I'm a girl. You think that means I should

probably be less than, right?"

"I didn't say that."

"But you imply it."

He shrugged, glanced at her then continued working away. "Besides Lilith, and her crew, I haven't seen many women around here with a lot of heart. That's what I meant to say." He took a deep breath.

"Well, maybe I just don't like assholes," Beth said. He snorted. "What about you? I don't get it. You're one of them and yet you just killed four."

"Six actually. Two more before I ended up at the clinic."

"All over a girl?"

"Hey. She's not just... a girl." He paused, reflecting. "Shelby's something else. Smart. You know — but not so smart that she flaunts it. And attractive." He looked at Beth and she got a sense he was studying her, maybe even comparing. She looked away feeling uncomfortable.

"How old are you?" she asked.

"Twenty-one. You?"

"Eighteen. Just turned it a month ago."

"Huh."

There was awkward silence so she tried to use the time to learn a little about him. "How long you been with these guys?"

"Since I was sixteen. Yeah, myself and Bosley didn't exactly grow up in the all-American family. Well, maybe if you can call having a crack addict for a mother, and an absent father all-American. Maybe we just got lucky. Anyway, me and him hit the road together. Within a year we were involved with the Reapers. In the beginning it was good. Really good. It felt like a family, a brotherhood. Parties galore. Women with legs as long as…" He looked at hers and she narrowed her gaze. He got this amused look on his face. "It wasn't long before Bosley moved up through the ranks and he changed. Got this god complex. Instead of it being about burning rubber, it was about drug and gun running and well you know where that leads."

"So you're against that lifestyle. The drugs?"

"Never touched it. Seen too many die from it. I stick to my beer. It's not the lifestyle of being a biker I'm against, it's all the shit that goes with it. It eats away at your soul. Every day you feel a little less human. And the way I see it, that's all we've got." He stopped what he was doing. "When the lights went out, we were based over in Johnson City. Bosley had this… epiphany… you could say. Figured that if we took to the road and found a small town with few roads in and out, we could take it." He shook his head as if finding it ridiculous.

"And you were against that?"

"Surviving, no. Killing innocent people, yeah."

She chuckled.

"What?" he asked.

"A biker with a conscience. Seems ironic."

"So because I have tattoos, dress like this and ride a bike, you immediately associate that with killing people?"

"Biker gangs don't exactly have a clean reputation," she replied. He paused what he was doing and looked at her.

"No, you're right. But to brushstroke us all as criminals is a little harsh, don't you think?"

"Hey, if the boot fits."

He laughed. "What about you?" He continued pouring gas and she continued filling the bottles with rags. "Landon said you helped him on the mountain. That true?"

"Wouldn't be here if it wasn't."

"Your family dead?"

She locked eyes and nodded.

"Yeah mine too. Well, besides Bosley but he might as well be dead. It's been a long time since I saw the brother I remember." He sighed. "Crazy to think how quickly life can change with the power going down."

She nodded thoughtfully. "My father used to say that one day it would and when it happened only those who had learned to live without would survive, some would get used to it but most would struggle, turn upon family, friends, even lovers in order to survive."

He nodded and began collecting the bottles they had

in a crate that was originally used for beer. "So why are you traveling with Landon? Why Maine? Why not just stay where you were on that mountain?"

She shrugged. "I've asked myself that many times. I don't have an answer right now or at least one that I can put into words. I just know it's the right thing to do. He needs someone to watch his back."

"As do you," Robbie replied.

"I've got Grizzly."

"Your dog." He laughed. "Right." He gestured with his hand. "C'mon, let's go."

Cautiously they made their way out the back and worked their way around until they saw Landon peering over the edge. Beth called out to him and told him they would meet him on the ground. They stayed hidden in that alleyway, waiting for him behind a large industrial dumpster. The smell of rotten food was worse than the dead.

As they sat there waiting, Robbie turned to her. "I admire what you did. Takes courage. I just hope I can get

Shelby out. I think you'll like her. She's got heart. Like you." He cracked a smile and then Landon appeared.

"Ready?"

They hustled through the back streets. The crate of bottles clinked loudly as Robbie carried them. Landon piped up. "You should have brought a bell with you. Maybe we could make some more noise," he said sarcastically. "Please tell me you have a plan for what we're about to do?"

"Trust me."

"I did," Beth added but didn't expand on it. Landon looked at both of them as if he was missing a piece of the puzzle. Robbie had set the crate down a few streets back and given each of them two bottles and then jogged on. They arrived at the first building — an attorney's office. He lit the rag on each of their bottles and directed them where to throw them.

Beth threw hers through a window and it erupted in a ball of fire.

What came next was screams.

A man rushed out holding a rifle but was covered in flames. He fell on the ground and began rolling trying to put himself out. Robbie stepped in and fired a round into him before they hurried away. "Six more buildings to go," he said without an ounce of remorse. Although he came across as having a heart, Beth couldn't help but wonder. If he was willing to do this to those he'd been around for years, what would he do to strangers?

Chapter 16

A bright orange glow arced over Mountain City as buildings went up in a blaze of glory. Although Landon had his doubts about Robbie, he was beginning to think he wasn't as stupid as he made out to be. The focus had dramatically shifted. Bikers worked frantically to get their buddies out of buildings, others stood back in horror unable to do anything. All the while they slipped by unnoticed, just silhouettes in the night. The numerous fires had given them exactly the distraction they wanted.

Draw them out.

Draw them away.

Bosley will go for it, Robbie kept saying.

Crouched in the underbrush they sat back and watched as the few remaining bikers streamed out including Bosley. "Perfect. I told you. Let's go," Robbie said leading the way. They hurried toward the bar using the darkness to stay hidden. Making it to the door,

Robbie peered inside. "It's all good."

They slipped in and Robbie called out to Shelby.

* * *

Lilith watched them enter. She should have known that Robbie was helping them. Robbie had been the wild card in her back pocket. She'd played him like a fiddle, pitting him against his brother by using Shelby to create jealousy. A master manipulator, she knew the only way to really overthrow the Reapers was to work from the inside out. In her mind, Robbie was the weaker of the two. If she could turn him against Bosley while at the same time gaining his trust, it would only be a matter of time before Robbie ended his brother's life, and took over as the president of the biker club. From there she would impose her will on him and control not just the women but the men as well. So many nights, she'd mulled over what it would be like to call the shots, to have an army of people at her beck and call. She'd be a modern-day Cleopatra.

"We should tell Bosley," Ruby said, sitting beside her in the Jeep.

"No. I want to handle this myself."

"But Willow…"

"Bosley is impulsive. He'll kill her. We can use her."

Ruby snorted. "She's like a wild horse. She's not like the others."

"Every horse can be broken," Lilith replied, casting her a glance.

There were very few girls she trusted but Ruby was one of them. She'd proven herself as loyal and Lilith knew without a doubt, she would rather take a bullet for her than see Lilith go down. "Here's what I want you to do. Take the girls north of here. I don't want any of them heading down this way. I need to do this alone."

"But Lilith—"

"Alone," Lilith spat back.

The truth was she didn't want Ruby to know the cards she'd been playing behind her back. The only way their relationship worked was if she felt she could trust her.

"And if something goes wrong?" Ruby asked.

"Then you'll take over the reins. You've always had

your eye on the prize, have you not?"

"I couldn't do it," she replied.

"Ruby, you give me too much credit. The girls look up to you. Willow, she was pushy, impulsive like Bosley. That's why he liked her, but you… You're steady and strong like a boat carving through the water. I need you to do this for me."

Ruby nodded. "Consider it done."

Lilith got out of the Jeep, palmed a fresh magazine into her handgun and jogged off into the night heading for the bar. Of course she was taking a risk but Robbie had a mouth on him and loose lips could sink a ship. She hadn't come this far to have all she'd built taken from her. Bosley on the other hand would have just killed them all.

Upon reaching the bar, she looked inside and heard voices, she couldn't make out what was being said but she could tell it was Robbie. She slipped in and locked the door behind her then moved around the wall of the building towards the side exit to lock that as well. She needed a few minutes with them. Just enough time to speak to this girl. She kicked herself wishing she'd done so when Ruby had brought her back to the restaurant the first time but she didn't know what she was made of at that point.

Once the doors were locked, she worked her way into the bar area. Standing in the doorway she watched as Robbie held Shelby. Shelby was a gorgeous blonde, a little ditzy but someone that followed orders well. If Robbie only knew the truth. She admired their relationship but then on the other hand it sickened her because she hadn't known that kind of love. Every man that she'd met wanted to get into bed with her and then be gone by morning.

"How sweet," she said walking out of the shadows, gun aimed at the one person she knew he wouldn't want her to kill — Shelby. The girl reacted, bringing up hers, but Landon intervened. "Beth, no."

"That's right, Beth. Listen to Landon. Put the gun down."

"Lilith," Robbie said. "Is Bosley here?"

"No. I thought you and I could have a little heart to heart. Bosley would only get in the way." She took a seat on a stool at the bar.

"You want to lower the gun," Robbie said getting in front of Shelby.

"Ah, young love. So sweet. But would you really die for her, Robbie? Or better still would Shelby die for you?" She paused. "Shelby, come over here." Without hesitation she moved around Robbie and he tried to hold on to her but she pulled away.

"Shelby?" Robbie asked.

Lilith's gaze bounced between them and Beth. She was just waiting for her to try her luck. One bullet. That's all it would take. It would be a waste of talent but oh well. Shelby sidled up to Lilith and placed her hands on her shoulder. Lilith turned her face to kiss Shelby but kept one eye on Robbie.

"I don't get it," Robbie said.

"Of course you don't. But let me ask you something. Where were you planning on going? I thought we had a deal?"

"We did. Things changed."

"No. That wasn't in the agreement. You were meant to kill him."

"I nearly did but…"

"But…?" she said leaning forward.

"Look, Bosley might have gone off the rails but he's still my flesh and blood."

"And Shelby? What is she? Chopped liver?"

"What?"

In an instant, Lilith lifted her arm and shot one round into Shelby's head. The girl dropped and Robbie screamed, rushing forward only to have her point the gun at him. "I wouldn't if I was you."

"You bitch."

"Um. That stings," she said.

"I'm gonna fucking kill you."

She chuckled. "And after we shared a bed together." She tutted. "So disappointing."

"What the hell do you want?" Beth asked.

"Ah, isn't that the question? What do I want," she said keeping her gun on Robbie whose hand was just itching to grab that piece in the front of his waistband. "It's quite simple. You."

"Me?" Beth replied.

"Don't act so surprised. You might fool others with that young girl's façade but I can see what you are below it all."

"Yeah? And what's that?"

"A survivor. Just like me. Just like all these girls. You belong here."

"You're insane," Beth replied.

"Oh come now, that's not a way to start a long-term relationship." She nudged towards Shelby's corpse. "Especially now we have an opening." She made her way over but stood out of reach. "Here's what I'm going to do for you. You value this man's life, yes?" Beth didn't reply as Lilith gestured toward Landon. "Yes or no?" she asked in a demanding tone.

"Yes."

"You want him to live, to make it back to Maine alive. Well there is only one way that's going to happen. I can get him out of this town. Away from Bosley. Away from being buried two foot under but I want something in exchange."

"I can get them out," Robbie said, cutting her off.

"Like you could kill your brother?" she said, shooting him a glance. She snorted when he didn't reply. "That's what I thought." She looked back at Beth but her eyes kept shifting between Landon and Robbie, expecting them at any second to go for their guns. "So? Your life or his. Decide."

"Lilith," Robbie said.

"Shut up."

"But I…"

Before he could finish, she squeezed a round at him then brought the gun back at Beth as she pushed forward, a flawed attempt at taking her down. The barrel of Lilith's gun pressed against Beth's forehead while she tried to bring up her weapon. "I wouldn't do that."

To the left of her, Robbie squirmed around on the floor. "You shot me. You fucking shot me."

"That I did. Be happy you're still alive."

He was gripping his shoulder. She'd purposely fired just above the heart. Some people only listened when pain was involved.

"So? What's it gonna be?"

Beth scowled. "Why would you want me to be a part of your group?"

"Why wouldn't I?" She laughed. "Look at what you have done already. That's quite a feat for a young girl. I can use that. Hone it. Come on. You don't want to be out there on the trail."

"The trail?"

She motioned to Landon. "Oh he told me all about it. You're heading for the Appalachian Trail. Trust me, Beth. It's safer here with me than it is out there. I can protect you from Bosley but out there, you are a heartbeat away from chewing on a bullet. Trails at the best of times aren't places for young women, and with all that's happened, nope, it's not a good place. And besides, without me you aren't getting out of here." She glanced at Robbie. "You think he's getting you out? You're mistaken. His loyalty to his brother runs deep. He promises a lot but fails to deliver. But me. I'm good for my word, aren't I, Robbie?"

Just as she turned her head for a second, Beth slapped the gun. It went off, firing a round into the floor as Beth kicked Lilith in the gut causing her to fly backwards and lose her footing. "Go. Go!" Robbie said scrambling to his feet and throwing himself on top of Lilith to prevent her from getting a round off at them. Landon and Beth hurried for the door while Lilith wrestled for control. Her gun went off three times in random directions as Robbie held on for dear life. Beneath him she saw Beth and Landon burst out of the door into the night.

Robbie smashed her hand against the floor until she released the gun and then he gripped her throat with both hands and began squeezing.

"Die. Bitch!"

Her peripheral vision started to go black. A few more

seconds and she would pass out. Taking her knee she slammed into his nuts and he groaned in pain but held on. She did it again, then again until his hands released and she shoved him off. Both of them scrambled for the gun like two crabs in sand hurrying to enter the ocean. She was inches away from grabbing it when he stuck a knife in her leg. Lilith wailed and collapsed only to have him snatch up the gun. "Now Robbie. What I did was for your good and mine."

"Shut up. You're just like him."

"No. I'm not. Why do you think I wanted him dead?"

Robbie fired a round into her thigh. She let out a pitiful cry, grasping her leg as blood slipped through her fingers.

"Shelby did nothing to you. Why? Why did you kill her?"

Lilith's tears turned to laughter. "She didn't even like you. What she did, she did for me."

"Don't lie!" he bellowed.

"Robbie, what you do now will—"

The gun went off and the light blinked out.

* * *

Robbie staggered back looking at Lilith's dead body. He brought a hand up to his shoulder and groaned in pain before making his way around the bar and unscrewing the cap off some bourbon and pouring it over his wound, and then taking a swig. His eyes darted to Shelby. Had she set him up? Used him like a tool? He would never know now. He brought the gun up to his head, contemplating shooting himself. *Pull it. Pull the damn trigger and it will be all over.* No more pain. No more anguish over Shelby's death. No more questions troubling his mind. What hope was left? The world had turned to shit and his life had gone down with it.

He took another swig of bourbon and sat on a stool looking at Lilith. He knew Lilith was playing him, and that was one of the many reasons why he wanted to leave but one thing she was right about — he couldn't leave without Shelby. Robbie screamed, emptying his lungs as he dropped to his knees and brought the gun to his head again. He was as good as dead anyway.

There on his knees, his thoughts shifted to Beth. The way she smiled at him. The way Landon had trusted him. Hope was hard to find nowadays but he'd felt it with them even if it was temporary. *Maine.* It was foolish to think he or they could reach it. It was over a thousand miles away. Lilith wasn't lying when she said that heading onto the trail was a bad decision. Rumors had swirled that groups had taken to the forests, trails and mountains to try and survive. Not all those groups were the helping kind.

Bosley had gone off the deep end and taken others with him.

Was there still hope for him?

He'd wanted to believe there was but his actions towards Shelby, and the town, said otherwise. The reality was the brother he knew was long gone, swallowed up by hate and anger. He would do better to not be alive.

He sighed and winced. He ran his hand into his jacket and felt the back of his shoulder. The bullet had gone straight through. Was this how it would end? Taking a bullet and bleeding out in some shithole in the middle of Tennessee? He'd done a lot of bad things with his life. If there was something good he could do before he died, it was now. Robbie slipped off the stool, gripping his shoulder and hurrying towards the door. He pushed out and made his way around the building. Seeing several bikers heading his way he called out to them. "Get Bosley. Lilith is dead in the bar."

The look of shock on their faces said it all as they took off to get him. Meanwhile, he staggered back into the tree line and found what remained of the Molotov cocktails. There were four left. It would have to do.

Under the cover of night, he watched as Bosley returned with the others and they streamed into the bar. He waited until the last one was in before hurrying out, a gun in one hand, the other carrying the crate with four bottles remaining. The gasoline mix sloshed out of the bottles as he tried to hold it with his bad arm. Reaching the door he set the crate down and picked up one of the cocktails, lit it and tossed it at the door, followed by another. He hurried around to the side exit and did the same, then positioned himself at the corner of the building and waited. Flames crept up the sides of the building setting fire to the wood structure. One by one, bikers tried to escape only to be cut down in a hail of bullets.

They eventually stopped trying to leave and the rest succumbed to smoke and flames.

On his knees, tears filled his eyes.

As he got up to leave, he heard movement behind him.

Stealing a glance over his shoulder, he looked upon five women, one of whom was Ruby. No words were exchanged and he knew what was coming next. A gun erupted, echoing in the valley.

Chapter 17

Mornings represented one thing to Jake — coffee, and there was no shortage of it. Long before the power went out, he'd purchased six months' worth of his favorite beans because the stores would often sell out so quickly of the brand he liked. It was just easier to scoop up multiple bags and stock up. He now wished he'd done the same with food. How hard would it have been to purchase an extra can of tuna, or peanut butter and keep it in storage for a rainy day? He was always throwing away the flyers that offered crazy deals like buy one get the second one at half price. Regrets were a big part of his daily life after the outage. He'd prepared for many things in life except the collapse. It seemed almost foolish. Car insurance, life insurance, pet insurance, dental insurance, health insurance; the world tried to prepare us for the worst-case scenario and yet not once had he been taught about being prepared to survive this.

He sighed inwardly, downed the remaining drop from his cup and screwed the lid back on the thermos as the sun was rising that morning. "Here, you want some?" he said handing it to Max. Over the past few months he'd noticed the way he'd withdrawn. The few times his mother had managed to get him to talk since that fateful night, he would just say he missed his father and Ellie but they knew it went deeper than that. No seventeen-year-old kid could kill two people and get up from it unaffected. Sara thought he was suffering from a mild form of PTSD. It was possible. The local doctor would have prescribed some meds if they could get their hands on any. The problem was the pharmacy had been looted in the first two months.

"Mom says I shouldn't."

"Hey, no one died from a cup of coffee." He paused and frowned. "At least I don't think so." Max let out a chuckle. It was the first time Jake had heard that in quite a while. "Hey, you smiled." The grin vanished. "You know, Max, it's okay to laugh. What you went through wasn't your fault."

"I know."

"No, I don't think you do. I think you're still blaming yourself in some ways. Your mother is worried."

"Can we drop this?" he said.

Jake studied him and nodded. "Sure. Well, come on, give me a hand setting this up." They had ventured into Witherle Woods that morning to set up snare traps to catch small animals. While it was good to fish and that wouldn't stop, all of them were growing tired of eating the same food. He figured they could catch a rabbit, squirrel or a ground-dwelling fowl like a quail or grouse using a few snares.

"So where did you learn about this?" Max asked as they trudged through the woods looking for a good location. It was key to be patient and look for nests and holes in trees along with trails in the underbrush that smaller animals were traveling.

"My father. He was into hunting. I never really was but I went along with him when I was younger."

"So you think this will work."

"I've yet to see it not," he said pointing ahead. "There. That tree. You see the hole that goes up into the tree? Looks like a squirrel could go up into it. There is a strong probability of catching one if we set it up, right here," he said dropping down in front of it. He shrugged off the backpack he was carrying and pulled out a pair of gloves.

"First key is to make sure you reduce the amount of scent that gets on the trap. No point setting it up only to have the squirrel smell your grubby hands." He slipped on a fresh pair of outdoor gloves. "Okay, next you need a strong, thick stick. You want to make sure it's long enough so you can bang it into the earth and create some real resistance. When an animal is fighting for its life, you don't want it pulling the stick out of the ground." He searched around and found one. He used a hatchet to chop off a piece that was the right length and he brought it back and showed Max. "Now you can use paracord or wire for this. Either one works fine." Max watched intently as he showed him how to sharpen the ends of the stick so it would go in the ground. As he worked away, he continued telling him what to do. "If you use wire to catch a squirrel, my father would always recommend a twenty-four or twenty-six gauge wire." He pulled a piece of cord out and chopped it off using his knife, then created a notch in the wood around the stake so the wire would embed into the wood and not slip. "Okay, just tie it off like this," he said, sniffing hard. "Now on the other end we will make the noose. Just be sure to have the noose about one hand away from the stake." He demonstrated by holding the stake up with the wire wrapped around it and putting his hand out like a flag flapping in the breeze. "Make sure the noose is about the size of a fist in width and it slides nice and easy. There has to be enough room but not too much." He handed it to him. "We'll make about five of these and disperse them through the woods. Hopefully by tomorrow, we'll have something."

"A squirrel?"

"You never ate that?"

"No. You don't get squirrel at a fast food restaurant."

Jake laughed. "You're right about that. But desperate times call for desperate measures and trust me, it doesn't taste that bad. It's kind of like chicken."

Max screwed his nose up and Jake chuckled. "If Ellie was here you wouldn't get her to eat it. She loves squirrels."

"Does she?"

He nodded and his smile faded.

"You miss her, don't you?"

"Her and I used to fight like cats and dogs but since she's been gone, it's just weird. I walk by her empty room expecting her to slam the door or call out to mom but it's just silent."

"I'm sure she's fine, Max. He's probably moving heaven and earth to get back here."

"Did you know him?"

"Not personally. Your mother, yeah. Since we were kids but I guess your father and I never really had the chance to get to know each other."

"You'd like him. He's fun. When he's not working."

"Did he ever teach you about this kind of stuff?"

"Hunting?" He laughed. "No. You couldn't get my father out in the wilderness. Bugs. He hates them."

"He flies planes but he hates bugs?"

"Yeah, crazy, huh?"

Jake smiled and continued by taking it over to the tree and banging the stick into the ground and clearing a path for the animal. "Okay, so extend out the noose. Check again that it's wide enough. Use your fist." He inserted his fist into it. "Next we need to set it around four fingers above the ground. Make sure it's securely anchored with twigs to support the loop, and that's it!" he said. "You've learned how to make your basic snare."

"But where's the incentive?"

"What do you mean?"

"You think the squirrel will just stick its head in there without some bait? Don't we need some nuts or something like that?"

Jake pulled out of his pocket a small tobacco tin and

popped the lid off. Inside was a small amount of peanut butter. "Don't tell your mother I took this. But you're right. It helps to have something to lure it in." He took a smear of peanut butter no bigger than the end of his finger and placed it on a stick just in front of the snare. They then went through the process of setting up a few more snares just in case an animal tried to go around it.

"One more I want to show you. If you don't want to do this, simply create three or four nooses of wire and attach them along a thin branch that a squirrel might navigate along, like that one over there," he said pointing to a branch that dipped down. "We will set up nooses upright and then smear some peanut butter on the branch in the space between the nooses. Now the squirrel will come along that branch and even if it manages to get around the first noose, the second or third usually will get it."

"And then you come back the next day to find a squirrel hanging off?"

"Bingo." He pulled a face. "I know it's a little morbid

but man has been doing this for years. Those beef patties you eat from your favorite fast food restaurant came from an animal that was caught and slaughtered. It's all about survival."

"Ellie would say, eat vegetables."

"Ah, she's a vegetarian?"

"She thinks she is but I've yet to see her turn down a Big Mac."

They both laughed. It was good to see him smiling again. Even though he would catch himself doing it and look serious again, it was a positive sign.

They rose to their feet and looked at the snares they'd set up.

"Any others?" Max asked.

"Traps and snares?"

He nodded.

"Yeah, the one I just showed you is pretty effective at catching birds as well as squirrels. Then you got spring snares, baited snares, leg snares, roller spring snares, double spring snares, deadfall traps and well don't get me started on fish traps. Though I will show you that. If anything ever happens to me or your mother, you should know this stuff."

"You like her, don't you?" Max said looking away.

"Your mother? Yeah. She's a good woman. Kind. Deserves to be taken care of."

"I agree but that's my father's job. Not yours," he said then walked away. Jake kind of figured the topic would eventually come up. He'd seen the way Max had given him the evil eye in the first few months at the Manor. Even more so at night when they were drinking wine and laughing. "My father is coming back. He'll be back real soon," he said over his shoulder.

"Yeah. He will."

He didn't want to push things or say anything that would rock the boat. In all honesty he'd forgotten about Landon. He'd seen the photos around the house but had turned them around or slipped them down into a sofa. It was stupid but he didn't like to feel he was under the watchful eye. The truth was he hadn't made a move on

Sara and he wouldn't. That wasn't his way. And if she wanted him to leave, he would. But it was her idea to have him stay in the house. Okay, Jake knew he had kind of pushed things by showing up with his tent but he was genuinely worried about her.

As they meandered through the woods setting up different traps, Max shut down and stopped talking as much. It didn't matter what he said, nothing worked.

At one point Max jogged ahead towards a steep bluff near Blockhouse Point. There was a stone wall that overlooked the bay. He hurried over to it and made Jake nervous. "Hey Max, hold up."

Max hopped over it and stopped just short of the stony edge. He looked down and pointed. "Jake. Jake!"

Out of breath, Jake caught up with him. "Seriously. What's the hurry?"

"What's that?"

Jake climbed over the stone wall and looked down and squinted. At first he just thought it was a pile of clothes, and then he saw a hand. Badly decomposed but it was a hand, nonetheless. "Stay here." Jake carefully made his way down the incline using roots and branches to support him. It took him a good five minutes to get down safely but when he made it, he placed a hand over his mouth. The smell of the dead body was foul. Flies were buzzing around it and it was clear small animals had already begun to nip away at the flesh.

He'd overheard the conversation Sara had with the deputy.

Women going missing.

One that had turned up dead.

He backed away and made it to the top of the bluff.

Jake guided Max away but not before looking back at it one final time. He couldn't tell who the woman was as the face was buried in the undergrowth, but either she'd fallen over the edge or someone had dumped her there. A sick feeling stirred in his gut. Looting was one thing, killing people took things to a whole new level.

"Jake. About what I said," Max muttered as they walked back through the woods to the Manor. "For what it's worth, I'm pleased you're at the house, if only for mom's sake."

He smiled and placed a hand on his shoulder. He wanted to reassure him but how could anyone do that now? With every passing month, the situation was becoming more dire.

Chapter 18

Thunderclouds spewed their wrath, clobbering them with huge raindrops at the break of day. It was like Mother Nature herself was against them reaching Maine. The weather was demoralizing only adding to their discouragement. To avoid being followed or having further problems with townsfolk, they'd avoided Damascus entirely and gone a slightly different route. They headed north of Mountain City, crossed a creek and stepped onto the Virginia Creeper Trail which was an old railroad bed that ran almost parallel to the AT. From there they picked up the Appalachian Trail twelve miles in, where the two trails reached the same spot. Every hundred yards or so, Beth would glance at white blazes painted on trees or rocks and mumble to herself, then press on. Landon learned that the vertical bars that were six inches tall marked the trail. They existed to ensure hikers didn't get lost even though according to Beth they still did, but it wasn't common.

Conversation between them had diminished but it was to be expected; both of them desperately needed sleep, food and shelter, and they hadn't stopped hiking since leaving the horrors of Mountain City.

He considered himself fortunate to be alive.

While they hadn't stuck around, they had seen smoke rising from the bar in the distance. Landon felt a twinge of regret leaving Robbie behind but he had a feeling that he wouldn't have come with them now that Shelby was dead.

Covered from head to toe in ultra-lightweight packable rain jackets they trudged on with only the sound of the wilderness as company. A flock of birds broke from a tree as they rounded a bend. Beth and Grizzly were far ahead of Landon. She'd stop every ten minutes and wait for him to catch up but it was clear he was slowing them down.

"How much farther?" he asked. "We should stop for breakfast."

"I don't want to risk it. Lost Mountain Shelter isn't far

from here. If we can reach that we can stop for a few hours."

Not far? She'd already told him it was roughly sixteen miles from Damascus. The weather had got the best of him. Irritated, he'd begun arguing with her about stopping.

"C'mon. I don't think anyone's following, Beth. No one would be insane enough to soldier on through this weather except us." He grimaced. It wasn't just his thighs that were burning, it was his feet, they were killing him. He was sure he had more blisters. The pitter-patter of rain was a constant as was the slopping of their boots as they trudged through a sheet of groundwater. He looked up at the skies. Even though it was morning the sky was a solid black with dark clouds, and a hard wind was driving rain into his face stinging his cheeks.

"If we pitch a tent there is a chance of flooding."

"But you said you saw a few stealth spots."

Stealth spots were areas that weren't clearly visible and were often clear of trees. Beth had told him that to avoid flash flooding she tended to pitch a tent on the top of hills or ridges. They might be exposed to the wind but the chances of getting flooded out were slim to none.

"My feet are killing me."

"Didn't you put on those nylon socks?"

It was a trick to avoid blisters by reducing friction. It required inserting your feet in two pairs of nylon socks, then if any rubbing occurred it would only happen between the layers of nylons.

"No. When did you tell me that?"

Beth stopped walking and looked back. "Let me guess, your socks are soaked?"

"Well, yeah."

"Great." She was carrying a small branch with her at the time. She shook her head and tossed it into the creek nearby and turned and kept walking. Landon stood there for a second or two then hurried to catch up.

"I need to air out my feet."

"You'll do it at the shelter."

He grumbled and they continued on. A few more

miles and they made it to Lost Mountain Shelter. The Appalachian Trail had roughly 250 garage-size shelters that were spread about a day's hike apart along the trail. More often than not they were filled with hikers, of course that was before the blackout. The aged log shelter had a lean-to style with one wall open to the elements and a picnic table out front. Landon shrugged off his backpack and tossed it on the table before laying back on the floor of the shelter. He lay there looking up at the ceiling and saw a spider scamper across the wood. "Oh no. No, no."

"What is it?" Beth asked whirling around looking disturbed.

He shot out of the shelter, pointing up. "I'm not sleeping in there."

"Why?" she said, confused.

"Take a look."

Beth frowned as she entered the shelter and looked up. "What am I looking at?"

"A tarantula."

A smile formed on her face and then she burst out laughing. "That tiny spider?"

"Tiny? Are you looking at the same thing?" he said hurrying over and glancing in before quickly backing up. "That's it. Screw that."

"Are you joking?" she asked.

"What? I don't like creepy crawlies."

"But you're a grown ass man."

"And you don't like heights."

"But you fly planes thousands of feet in the air."

"And you live high up on a mountain. Yes, I get the irony of it but we all have things we don't like. Screw that, I'm pitching the tent."

She stepped out and went over to her pack to unload the MSR stove. "Sleeping in a tent won't be much better. You must have expected this. You'll see them every day out here. It's the woods. Besides that one isn't a black widow or brown recluse spider. Now those you have to be worried about."

"What?"

She was hunched over her bag when she looked at him. "Black widows. Brown recluses. You get them out here. Well, mostly the female black widows as the brown aren't native to Virginia. Though I was told by a friend that her buddy got bitten. So who knows. Though I think it's the rats and mice you should be worried about." She grinned as if finding pleasure in taunting him.

Landon threw up a hand, his imagination going into overdrive. "I get it. Okay. I get it," he said making his way over to a clearing to pitch the tent. His skin was crawling at the thought of waking with a big spider on his face, or worse having one crawl into his mouth or ears. Some might say his fear of all things crawly wasn't rational but it had started when he was a kid and his father had taken him out camping for the first time and he awoke to find spiders all over the tent. Then he had one bite him. Of course Sara would take every chance she got to wind him up.

"Need a hand?" Beth asked.

"I'm fine."

"Look, I don't mean to embarrass you. I get it. Spiders can be a bit creepy but that's all part of coming out into the woods. You have to be prepared for the dangers. In all honesty though the biggest threat against us out here is ticks. Nothing worse than coming down with Lyme disease."

"Oh, how pleasant," he said pulling out the tent and trying to figure out how to set it up. "And there was me thinking you were about to say bears, rattlesnakes and deranged, inbred hillbillies."

"You never know, we might come across those." She burst out laughing. It was good to see her laughing even if it was at his expense. "No, in seriousness, deer ticks are pretty bad the further east we go. I should have warned you about that. You'll need to check your skin every day. Usually they have to be on you for more than thirty-six hours before there is any real risk, though most people don't know when they land. So make sure you keep your arms and legs covered and spray your clothes with that can of Permethrin."

"What can?" he asked.

"The one we packed."

He looked in his bag and started pulling out items and sure enough it wasn't in there. "Where did it go?" she asked.

"Oh man. I bet you any money Robbie pulled it out and used it in his town plan. He was rooting through my bag for food. I gave him some jerky and…"

"You gave him food?"

"He was hungry. He'd been eating dog food."

"How much food you got left?" She took a look and sighed. "Great! That means we'll have to stop at a town sooner than we thought." She tossed his bag down and went to walk away.

"Why? You've got a bow. You're a great shot. We could trap a few rabbits and…"

She turned and looked at him. "If we were sticking around, yes, but we've got to keep moving. Hunting requires time. We don't have time. And I don't even like the idea of being this close to Mountain City."

"We are miles and miles away," Landon said stabbing his finger in the direction they'd come. "And Lilith is dead, the bar went up in flames with Bosley inside. What's the problem?"

"Ruby."

He studied her. "Now you're being paranoid."

"Am I? It was her that came after us when I killed Willow."

"That's because they had some deal with those assholes in Mountain City."

She ignored him and went about getting her little nook in the shelter set up. There was an outhouse nearby, and the closest water source was a creek not far away.

Rain continued to beat down turning the ground to mush. A small stream of water ran past him as he struggled to get his tent set up. Somehow, he managed to get a rod tangled up and he tossed it down in frustration and yelled into the sky, shaking his fist. "Why. Why her! I hate you." His anger towards God had reached a new level. He would have given anything to have taken her spot.

He glanced over at Beth who was staring at him. She reached into her bag and dug around and held up what looked like a small bag. "Here. You can use my bivy sack. It'll keep the spiders off you. Don't bother with the tent. Come on."

"Bivy?"

"I didn't have one for both of us. It's a small lightweight alternative to carrying a tent." She laid it out and showed him how to set it up. It basically looked like a sleeping bag or a giant windsock with a large space at one end that was made from bug netting material so the face wasn't smothered and bugs didn't get in.

"Geesh, now that's what I'm talking about."

"It'll keep the bugs off you."

"Thanks, Beth."

He kind of felt like a fool for bellowing into the sky but even after four months the grief of losing Ellie was still as fresh as the day of the crash. Beth went about getting some breakfast together while he went to relieve himself. He dug around in his bag for the small bathroom baggie. He was the only one who had brought it with him as Beth said she could identify leaves that worked just as well. She'd tried to teach him up at the cabin what plants were good for what but he got confused after five. And besides, knowing his luck he would probably misidentify and reach for some poison oak and spend the rest of the trip with a raw ass. *No thanks.* Anyway, with limited space in their bags and regular toilet paper being too bulky, she opted to have him carry toilet paper tablets. And the only reason she agreed was because they had multiple uses: they could be used for toilet paper, hygiene, cleaning wounds, bandages, fire starting and feminine hygiene. He'd never seen them before. Landon had to admit it was a cool invention. They reminded him of white chalky Tums. The trick was simple, he dunked one into water for less than a second and it instantly expanded allowing him to pull apart the compressed towel. They were strong, biodegradable and absorbent which was a bonus. He'd already taken a couple and soaked them so they were ready for him to use.

"Where you going?"

"To take a dump."

"But the outhouse is over there."

"So are probably a million spiders," he muttered.

"Well just remember to go two hundred feet from the stream or trail to bury it. Oh, and that's around eighty paces."

He shook his head. "Like it really matters now."

"I heard that," she said gesturing to nature. "This is all we have left. You don't want to go ruining the water sources. With all this flooding, your crap could end up in the stream."

Landon grumbled under his breath as he ventured into the woods to find a spot. His eyes scanned the trees and underbrush for small or large animals. After the shit luck they'd had, he wouldn't have been surprised to find himself staring down a cougar just when he was about to do a number two.

"Oh hey, can you get some water while you're out

there?"

He jogged back and collected a Platypus bag and hurried as his stomach was doing flips. First things first. How many paces? *Ah screw it if I don't go now, I'm going to...* Landon dropped his pants and squatted as the heavens above rained down on him. And people do this for fun? he thought. Crazy. The idea of venturing into the wilderness to relax had never really appealed to him unless it was in an RV. There were just too many dangers. It was a bit of an oxymoron really as at any point in his flying career he could have found himself having to do an emergency landing and getting stranded, but in his mind the odds of that happening were slim. But purposely heading into the wilderness. That was insane. As he sat there finishing up, he purposely had to shift his mind to Sara and Max otherwise he didn't think he would make the journey. Over a thousand miles remained and in the short span of a few days they'd already touched death's door. How much worse could it get?

Fortunately no cougar showed up.

Landon made his way over to the stream, trampling over new growth. The earth below him was soaked even though a large amount of it was covered in moss and leaves. He crouched down and lowered the dirty side of the Platypus gravity filter into the stream and filled it up. The water was freezing as he dipped his hand into it. Just as the bag was filling, he heard a branch or twigs snap behind him.

Landon froze.

His head turned ever so slightly hoping it was Beth.

It wasn't.

Chapter 19

Castine's town manager, Teresa McKenna, flipped the pages of his report. It was quiet in the town hall office, only a ticking clock could be heard. Sam glanced at Carl sitting in the plush chair beside him. He was biting his nails and spitting them onto the floor. The office was cramped, nothing more than a table, three leather chairs and a cream-colored filing cabinet. "And you're sure this woman is Danielle Jenkins?" she asked looking over her glasses at him.

He nodded. "We had the family come down to the morgue to identify her."

The temporary morgue in Castine wasn't exactly a morgue, so to speak. They were using one of the huge boats at the dock. It kept the bodies out of sight, off limits to the public, and it enclosed the smell. The two women weren't the only ones there. In the months that followed the blackout there were those who had taken their lives, and some who were brutally killed. Some still hadn't been identified so their bodies were kept there for a short while until the town buried them.

"So two of the missing women have shown up dead in Witherle Woods, one buried, the other found at the bottom of a bluff. And you think the third is somewhere in there?"

"It's a guess right now. We were hoping to get some assistance from locals today to perform a sweep of the woods," Carl interjected. "Bring an end to this."

"No, that's not a good idea."

"Why not?" Carl asked.

She removed her glasses and placed them in front of her, then sat back in her black leather seat. Teresa was in her mid-fifties, round faced, dark curly hair, slightly overweight with rosy cheeks. She was wearing a white shirt and a pencil skirt. "People in town are already traumatized enough by this event. We don't want to create more panic. If they think that someone is murdering people for fun or for supplies, we could have a riot on our hands."

"What do you expect us to do then… pretend this is not happening? We have to make sure the remaining members of the town are on high alert, maybe employ a neighborhood watch group that can circulate residential homes in the day and evening."

"Listen, Sam, we already had a meeting to discuss deputizing. You were very specific about the kind of people you wanted to work with and I agreed. But where did those people go? That's right, they appear to have left town. No one wants to do this job. And anyone who does, I'm a little skeptical about their reasons. Placing power in the hands of unknowns can lead to disastrous results."

"We might not have a choice," Sam said. "At some point we have to trust this community."

"And yet it's very possible someone from the community is doing this, yes?"

He waited for a second before nodding.

She got up and went over to her bag and took out a

bottle of water, twisted the top off and guzzled it down. "Trust is at an all-time low, deputy." Carl nudged Sam as if expecting him to say something. Fresh water, at least water that didn't need purifying, was hard to come by. Sam waved Carl off. It was probably taken from Teresa's own cache. Everyone was entitled to their own. She took a seat. "I had several families come into my office over the last few days to express their concern over fights breaking out, domestics and theft. Disappearances right now are just not the priority. As much as I would love to give closure to this third family, we just don't have the resources. You should know that better than anyone. I need you both here every day to deal with these matters as they arise. And lately you have been absent."

"So you just want us to turn the other cheek, is that right?" Sam asked.

"No. I want you to go out and do your job."

"What do you think I'm trying to do?" he shot back.

"I understand. But scouring the woods is a waste of time that we don't have."

"You mean, you don't have. As it would be down to you to deal with these people."

She glared at him. "Deputy. I don't need to be here. Let's get that clear."

"And nor do we, lady," Carl said. "Let's get that clear."

She pursed her lips and inhaled. "All I'm saying is people need to see your face. Give them a sense that law and order is still alive and well in Castine. That's what people need to see. Like what you did yesterday with the attack on Gene Sommers. Tackle those day-to-day issues, nothing more."

"Is that what you promised the families?" Sam asked thinking Teresa was full of shit.

"I told them we are doing the best we can under the circumstances."

"And what did they say?"

"They didn't say anything. They stormed off."

"I wonder why." Carl rolled his eyes.

Sam sighed and ran a hand over his face. "Look, I care about this town as much as you do. I don't want to see it go to hell in a handbasket but if we don't put a stop to whoever is killing, we won't have a town to help."

Teresa took her seat. "How many people do you know that can help with scouring the forest?"

Sam pulled a face thinking of a few. It was hard to know if they would be up for it. It wasn't that they were qualified but two of them had already been exposed to what they were looking for. "I have a couple in mind."

"Well if you could leave your friend here," she said in a non-enthusiastic way, pointing to Carl, "I'd be more than happy to agree to you taking today to scour the forest."

"Agree? Like we need your permission," Carl said. "We don't work for you. We work for the county."

"And this town is run by the county. So yes, you work for me," she said with a smug look on her face. "At least until..." she trailed off as if she was about to say something that might affect the future of the town.

"Until what?" Sam asked.

"Nothing. Anyway..."

The door opened and Heidi, her assistant, poked her

head in. "Teresa. We have a bit of a problem outside."

Sam and Carl rose to go and see what was happening. On the way down the hall, Heidi filled them in. "Just to warn you, some of them are armed."

Sam glanced at Carl. He knew what to do. He would collect a shotgun from the trunk of the Toyota parked at the rear of the building while he went to calm the rising storm. He burst out of the main doors into a throng of people that had gathered. There had to be eighty, maybe a hundred at a rough headcount. Most of them were men. The jeering, shouting and cursing was deafening. Sam elbowed his way through the crowd trying to get to the center and find out what was happening. They'd gathered on the street and over the heads of the people he saw someone throw a rope over a tree branch outside the home directly across from Emerson Hall.

"No government. No judge. No jury. What we do today is agreed upon by this community. All those in favor say aye!" The voice was familiar.

The crowd roared a reply, "Aye!"

"Get out of the way," Sam said, pushing his way to the front. As he managed to burst into the clearing, he saw a badly beaten black man lying on the ground. He didn't even look as if he was conscious.

"String him up, boys."

Sam's eyes bounced to Mick Bennington, a local fisherman and troublemaker. He was six feet of rippling tattooed muscle. A square jaw covered in a thick black beard with piercing black eyes that would make any man shudder. Today he was wearing a thick blue jean jacket with fur on the collar, T-shirt and faded jeans and his regular work boots. He rarely changed his wardrobe. Sam had been called out multiple times to a bar in town to break up fights between Mick and others. It was always the same. Someone gave him a dirty look. Someone spilled his drink. Fists flew and he'd land himself in jail sleeping off the alcohol.

Sam pulled his service weapon and fired a round into the air.

Heads turned.

Startled expressions.

Murmuring ensued.

"Bennington. What the hell is going on?" Sam said making a beeline for him.

"Stay out of this, deputy. The community has spoken and this man is getting what's coming to him."

"Who is he and what's his crime?"

"You don't get a say in this. String him up."

Sam rushed over to intervene, pushing back Dave Robson, another fisherman who was in the process of slinging a noose over the guy's head. "Back off!" Sam said. "Anyone touches this man you will…"

"You want to know his crime? He raped a sixteen-year-old girl, deputy."

"And your proof?"

Mick waved him off. "Ignore him. Get him up in the air."

Sam raised his gun at Dave and told him to back up, just as Carl squeezed through the crowd with a shotgun in hand. He backed him up, pointing at anyone who tried to get near Sam. The crowd looked as if they didn't care who they hung as long as they saw some form of justice. Sam couldn't believe it had got to this — taking matters into their own hands.

"This is not how we handle things!" Sam spat.

"No?" Mick asked. "Then tell us, deputy. How do you deal with a man like this?" he said spitting at the guy near Sam's feet. "What are you going to do... put him in a makeshift cell? Feed him three meals a day? Try to get him to change his ways?" He chuckled as he walked around speaking to the people. "Or maybe you want to get him before the judge and have him determine that he's insane, or this is a human rights issue that needs more time, or maybe there isn't enough proof and so you'll release him to rape again. Huh? Is that how you handle things? Because it seems to me that you aren't handling much of anything, and that includes the three missing women."

Sam stared back at him and Mick continued.

"Oh that's right. We already know about that. We

know about the two bodies found in Witherle Woods. We know you don't have a suspect, a lead, hell, you don't have shit!" The people around them got fired up and jeered. "The fact is law is defunct in this county. So step aside so we can give this man what he deserves and these people justice."

Mick stepped forward and Sam turned his gun on him. "You take one more step and I swear it will be the last you take."

Right then, pushing through the crowd, Jake came into view carrying a rifle. He lifted it at some of the men that were getting a little too close to the deputies. "Back up," he yelled. Sam glanced at him. He might have said something but he was actually glad to see someone back them up.

"You're making a big mistake, deputy," Mick said.

"Yeah, well that's for us to make and for all of you to get on with whatever the hell you were doing before this!" he said in a loud voice. "Go on. Go back home. We will take it from here."

There was a moment of reluctance then slowly the crowd thinned out and Mick shook his finger at Sam. "This isn't over." He turned and walked off with several of his buddies who looked over their shoulders at them as they carried the stranger into Emerson Hall and locked the doors.

"I appreciate what you did back there," Sam said to Jake as they took the man into one of the closest rooms and laid him down. "Carl, get me some water and a towel."

Carl shot off to get it.

"Yeah, well, I thought things were a little off-balanced."

"Lucky you were in the neighborhood."

"I had to swing by my place to make sure no one had broken in," he said looking at the stranger.

Sam chuckled. "An optimist."

"What?"

"You're worried that your business won't be ready to go when the lights come back on."

"You got to hold out some hope, right?"

"Right." He nodded.

"You know this guy?" he asked Sam.

"No."

"Doesn't look like a local. Man, they laid down one hell of a beating on him."

Sam wiped his brow with the back of his hand. "Yeah, that Mick Bennington is an asshole. Now I have him to deal with."

"You need more deputies."

He laughed. "Tell me about it."

Carl returned with the water and towel and Sam crouched beside the man and cleaned his face. His eyes were badly swollen, he looked as if someone had broken his nose, and several of his fingers. As he dipped the towel into the water for a second time, the man gasped then swung a fist, knocking Sam back. Carl and Jake held him down and told him he was safe. It took him a second to realize they weren't a threat before he relaxed.

"Where am I?"

"Emerson Hall. You got a name?" Sam asked wiping blood from his lip.

"Damar Washington. And you are?"

"Deputy Daniels, and this is my partner, Deputy Madden and—"

"Jake Parish," Jake said before Sam could say. Carl went over to the window to take a look outside and make sure the crowd was definitely gone.

"Where are you from?" Sam asked while the other two listened intently.

"Brooksville. I came over by boat to see how things were over here."

"Those men said you raped a girl, that true?" Sam didn't expect him to tell the truth if he had done it but he'd been a cop long enough to tell if someone was lying by the way they reacted.

"Rape? What are you talking about?"

"You have no recollection?"

"Like I said, I came over here by boat. The last thing I remember was walking down a street near the dock and some guys jumped me."

"Jumped you?" Carl asked. "Who?"

Damar shook his head. "They came at me from behind. I didn't see them."

Sam rose from a crouch and went over to Carl. "Now why would anyone jump a complete stranger?"

Carl immediately jumped to a conclusion that Mick was behind it. "He is racist."

"Maybe but still… there are too many things vying for our attention, survival for instance. Why waste your time beating up a complete stranger?"

"Let's pull Mick in and ask him."

"Easier said than done," Sam replied looking back at the stranger who was now talking with Jake. A confrontation with Mick was the last thing he wanted.

Chapter 20

In an instant, Landon wheeled around, his finger on the trigger ready to squeeze off a round. The two strangers' hands went up; cowering back, a look of shock. "Whoa, mister, we don't mean any trouble. We're just here for water," the guy said. Both of them were in their late-forties, the male had a dark, thick beard, and a bandanna wrapped around his neck, a green Riffraff shirt, brown shorts and hiking boots. The female had long blond hair, a purple Riffraff shirt and black shorts with similar style boots. "Sorry, we thought you heard us."

"You should be careful creeping up on people."

Landon lowered the gun and climbed up from the rocky water's edge, his hand still holding the gun tightly at his side. He still wasn't sure how safe he was. He nudged them towards the water and they moved past him and refilled their bottles. Neither one was carrying a rifle, or handgun at least that he could see.

"The name's Bear Whisperer, and this is Lost and Found," the guy said.

"What?" Landon asked, giving them a confused expression. "Bear Whisperer?"

The guy nodded. "Yeah, it's our trail names. What's yours?"

"I don't have one."

They looked at each other then tossed back an equally confused reply. "Everyone has one."

"Well not me," he said hooking up the Platypus gravity filter in a tree and watching as it filtered out the crap and drained into the second, clean bag. Landon kept a close eye on them as they continued to fill up. After Mountain City he wasn't taking any chances. "What the hell is a trail name, anyway?"

The woman chuckled. "Newbie alert."

"Give him a break." He looked back at Landon. "You must be new to hiking. The short and sweet answer is that it all started here, on the Appalachian Trail. With so many people hiking it was just an easy way to keep track of people by giving them a nickname. The names are usually related to either personality or history. For example mine came from our frequent encounters with bears. For some strange reason every time I've encountered an aggressive one, I've only had to speak to them and they wander off. No idea why. And Nancy here got hers after continually losing items and then finding them again." They both laughed as if reliving some shared joke. Once they had their bottles filled up, they climbed back up the steep embankment. "What about you? What brings you out this way?"

"Trying to get home."

"Ah, and where might that be?"

"Maine."

"Then you're heading in the right direction, though I would be careful out there. Lots of weirdos on this trail. I mean you get your fair share at the best of times but lately, with the power grid down, there's a number of people who have escaped to the trail and shelters. Not all of them are as friendly as we are."

"Is that so," Landon said, his eyes narrowing. "And where are you two heading?"

"Georgia. Yeah, this is the third time we've completed the AT. We opted to start in the winter this year from Maine. It wasn't long after the power grid went down."

"You were in Maine when it went out?"

"No, we were long gone by then. We only found out when we stopped in the town of Boiling Springs, Pennsylvania, to get supplies and there were none. You should have seen the place. It was a nightmare." Landon's eyes shifted to the woman who was rooting through her backpack. For a second, he thought the guy was making conversation to keep him distracted but when she pulled out a granola bar and tore the wrapper off, he relaxed.

"You camped nearby?"

"Lost Mountain Shelter," Landon replied.

"Ah, the same place we were heading."

"Convenient. Well you'll find there's plenty of space. We're just there to get a few hours' sleep and then continue on our way." The guy nodded; a creepy smile formed. "So you said your girlfriend's name is Nancy. And you?" Landon asked.

"Terry. But I prefer my trail name."

"I think I'll stick to Terry if you don't mind."

Terry glanced at Nancy and she shrugged.

Once the water was filtered, he began trekking back to the shelter. Landon let them walk just a few feet ahead, still unsure. There was no way of knowing who they were dealing with. They could tell he was a little on edge as Terry would tell him it was okay to put the gun away but he didn't. They made it out of the forest into the clearing and Beth was hanging a few pieces of clothing that were damp. She turned and immediately reached for her rifle. "It's okay, Beth!" Landon said.

"We come in peace," Nancy added, waving.

"Ah we're just in time for breakfast," Terry said making a beeline for Beth and extending his hand. "Terry, or you can call me Bear Whisperer, and you are?"

"Bluebird."

He grinned. "Ah, someone has a trail name. Your

friend here was telling me he doesn't have one. Hell I didn't even catch his real name." Terry sat down on the picnic bench and took a load off his back. His backpack seemed much larger than those they were carrying.

"Landon," Beth said. "His name is Landon."

"And what have you got cooking this morning then, Beth?"

"Oatmeal, raisins, sugar, powdered milk, cinnamon and nutmeg."

"Sounds delicious."

"Sorry, only enough for the two of us," she said.

He chuckled. "Hey, it's fine, we're actually doing pretty good, aren't we, Lost and Found?" Even Beth turned her head and frowned. It was weird, that was for sure. He continued. "Yeah, we came across some trail angels along the way and they sprinkled some of their trail magic."

"I hear the word trail one more time, I'm gonna shoot someone," Landon mumbled under his breath. Terry began pulling out of his bag granola bars, candy bars and soda pop. "Where did you find all that?" Landon asked.

"In a cooler. Oh, that's right, this is your first time on the trail. Well let me educate you. Trail magic can be as simple as a ride into town, a cold drink at the trailhead or offering someone a shower or bunk for the night, through to coolers found on the trail filled with candy bars and soda. With so few hikers this year, the last cooler we came across was still packed. We took the whole damn lot, didn't we, darlin'?" he said speaking to Nancy. She nodded and yanked off her boots to examine her feet. They looked in a pretty bad state, bandages wrapped around her ankles, two purple toes and a black nail made Landon grimace. Long-distance hiking was hard on the body.

"Here, catch." Terry tossed Beth a few candy bars, and some soda. She thanked him and put them in her bag. Landon brought the water over to Beth and she gave him this look, like are you sure about this? His eyes dropped to his gun and that was enough.

"Do either of you partake?" Terry said pulling out a

Ziploc bag of weed. They both shook their heads. He proceeded to make himself a joint. Five minutes later he continued peppering them with questions. "So you're his daughter?"

"No. We're just friends."

"So Landon mentioned you're heading to Maine. Is that where you're from?"

"North Carolina," she replied stirring the pot. Steam rose above it and Landon's stomach grumbled. In all the excitement and terror of their time in Mountain City he hadn't had much time to eat besides a few pieces of jerky and some summer sausage. "What about you two?"

"Georgia, though we had flown up to Maine to do the southbound trek. Never quite imagined it would go down like this."

"You were on the trail when it happened?"

"Yeah." Terry nodded, biting into a candy bar and washing it back with some soda.

"So what's it like out there?" Landon asked.

The smile went from Terry's face as well as Nancy's.

"Like hell. Word of advice. Stay away from the towns unless you really need to. It's terrible. Some towns have been burned to the ground. Planes have destroyed them; others have been overrun with gangs and criminals. We had to fight for our lives a few times." He reached over and scratched Grizzly under the chin. "Beautiful. What's his name?"

"Grizzly," Beth replied.

Tears welled up in Terry's eyes. "We had a dog with us — Old Buddy. A beautiful golden lab. Best dog I have ever had. He was attacked by a cougar. Didn't make it. Died protecting us though." Nancy walked over and placed a hand on Terry's shoulder, he looked at it before smiling. It was only then that Landon put the handgun back into its holster on his hip. He had a good sense about people and he could tell they weren't going to be trouble.

"As you're giving out advice, we have some for you," Landon said. "Stay away from Mountain City and Neva. All that's waiting there is a whole lot of trouble."

"Advice taken," Nancy replied.

A wave of tiredness hit Landon as he sat down and ate a bowl of oats. It had been the first time in over twenty-four hours that he'd felt safe enough to close his eyes. "I can't keep my eyes open any longer."

"I'll take the first watch," Beth said.

"Ah you don't need to do that," Nancy said. "You two get your heads down. We'll keep an eye out for trouble."

Although Landon was fine with that, mostly because at that point, he would have fallen asleep standing up, Beth looked less convinced.

"No, it's fine. I'm good," she said.

"Suit yourself, hon." Nancy wandered over to a firepit and went to start one. Beth jumped and rushed over to stop her. "No. It will create smoke."

"But darlin', you used a stove."

"It's not the same," Beth replied.

Landon understood; they didn't.

"You two really are spooked," she said, her eyes bouncing to Terry. Terry made a gesture with his head, and she returned to him. Exhausted, Landon removed his boots and coat and slipped into his sleeping bag inside the bivy and zipped it up. He looked up through the net and could still see the spider but felt a little less intimidated. He turned and glanced at Beth who was sitting at the picnic table with her rifle in hand. He knew as soon as he closed his eyes he'd be out like a light. He just needed an hour or two and he'd be set.

"You gonna be okay?" Landon asked.

"I'm fine. Go to sleep."

His eyelids fluttered, and closed, then opened. This repeated four times, each time he saw Beth at the picnic table and Terry and Nancy chatting.

"Well we really should get going." Those were the final words he heard before he drifted into oblivion.

* * *

Beth struggled to keep her eyes open as she leaned against her rifle. Terry and Nancy had left the camp twenty minutes ago. They genuinely seemed grateful for the company even though it was short-lived. Although

Beth desperately needed sleep, she had to stay awake. An hour. That's all he needs then he can take over and I can sleep, she told herself. The rustling of trees and the babble of the nearby stream lulled her to sleep and she kept abruptly opening her eyes and gasping. Beth slapped her cheeks a few times and took some of the water from her bag and splashed it on her face. The slap of cold jerked her upright. Even Grizzly was dozing, his head resting between his paws, his eyelids opened and closed revealing his bloodshot eyes.

The sounds of the forest brought back memories of her father. God, how she missed him. What she would have given to have him here. She glanced at Landon who was out like a light. He was snoring up a storm. She understood his grief, if it wasn't for him, she wasn't sure what she would have done. In some ways they had saved each other.

A few times, Beth drifted off and didn't realize until her eyes opened. Each time she would look around with a sense that someone was watching. At one point she got up

ALL THAT SURVIVES: A Post-Apocalyptic EMP Survival Thriller

and paced the perimeter of their campsite scanning for trouble. Eventually she returned to her spot and rested against her rifle.

The fifth time she fell asleep, she must have been out a while as when she came to the sun had shifted in the sky. She glanced at her watch and realized she'd been asleep for just over two hours. She turned and looked at Landon who was still asleep.

It was then she noticed something odd.

"Where's my backpack?"

She hopped off the picnic table and looked underneath. "It was here. Right near my feet." She looked over at Grizzly and he was still sleeping. "Grizzly. Grizzly," she said a few times but he didn't move. Fear shot through her as she rushed to his side and placed a hand on his chest and listened for breathing. He was breathing but was out cold. If she wasn't mistaken, he was sedated. A flash of memory, Terry giving the dog some food from a can. She hurried over to the trash can and she pulled it out and sniffed it as if thinking that would answer her question. Inside she noticed a fine layer of powder as if a tablet had been crushed.

"Shit. Shit!" she yelled, hurrying over to the bear pole where she'd raised the food up. It was gone. The bag was gone. "No. No. NO!"

She remembered Terry's backpack and how heavy it looked. No hiker with a lick of sense would have carried something as heavy as that. Had that food really been from a cooler they'd come across or had they stolen another hiker's bag? Bastards! She knew it was too good to be true. They came across all nice but it was an act. Just an act. Beth hurried over to the shelter and searched for Landon's backpack. It too was gone.

They had taken everything but the clothes on their backs, her rifle because she'd been leaning up against it, her hatchet which was attached to her waist, her bow and arrows and their handguns. She couldn't believe this was happening. They must have waited in the forest, watching them until she fell asleep and then crept in and took it right out from underneath their noses.

Beth rushed back to the shelter and unzipped the bivy. She shook his shoulders. "Landon. Landon! Wake up."

He began to stir, slapping his lips together and opening his droopy eyes.

"What's the matter?"

Through gritted teeth she spoke. "They took everything. Everything!"

Chapter 21

The thought of a deadly confrontation with Mick lingered in Sam's mind as he and a group of forty-six residents entered Witherle Woods that afternoon. Jake Parish had been an absolute godsend. Not only had he stepped in and backed them up when things were close to getting out of hand, but his connections with the community had given him a foot in the door that not even they could have managed. It had taken him a couple of hours to rally together the ragtag crew.

When they showed up outside Sara's home, Sam was more than impressed, he was elated. More boots on the ground increased the odds of success. Still, even with the additional support, finding Debbie Stevens, the third missing woman, in the 185-acre preserve packed with spruce, fir, pine and hardwood trees would be like scouring for a needle in a haystack.

Determined to make use of the limited daylight hours,

Sam had pinned a map to the wall inside the Manor and with a marker pen segmented sections of the woods focused around key areas such as Dyce's Head Lighthouse, and Shore Gun Batteries, No. 1, No. 2, Trask Rock, the Lookout, Moore's Hill and Forward Battery on the east side. It would take them all on a path across multiple trails, more specifically Indian Trail, a 1.4-mile loop that was commonly used by hikers.

He figured that would have been the easiest way in and out, and based on the location of the previous bodies, it seemed whoever was responsible wasn't going to great lengths to hide them.

Like any formal search, they would begin by creating bump lines that sectioned off areas in the forest as a place to start and stop. From there, one person at the end of a group of five would walk away from that bump line with a string, tie it to a tree and they would shift to the other side, turn and head back to the bump line, crossing their section of the woods until they had covered each grid. By the time they were done at the end of the day, the inside of the woods would resemble a spider web, allowing them to see which areas had been searched. Prior to doing this, Sam marked out the locations of the two women that had been found and gave each group a flare to fire into the air if they found Debbie.

Sam, Jake and Carl carried two-way radios and watched over a group of five to make sure a thorough search was conducted. Sara Gray was put in his group, giving him a chance to talk to her about how she was doing as they worked their way through the brush.

"Jake did a good thing today."

"Yeah, he's very helpful," she said.

Although they were sure Debbie was dead, they still had to treat her as someone who might have just got lost and injured, so throughout the forest people could be heard calling her name. Each of them used long sticks to move the brush and they worked a few feet apart. It was an arduous process that would take them all afternoon but he was determined to prove to Teresa that the community could be trusted to work together.

"It's good what you're doing. Trying to make a difference, I mean," she said.

"I wouldn't say it's that," he said. "It just my job."

Sara nodded. "But—"

"We're four months in," he said, saying what he thought she was about to say.

She smiled and he continued. "Yeah, I have thought about it myself. I guess a little part of me still believes that the lights will come back on again. And when they do, I don't think I could look myself in the mirror if I hadn't tried to help when people needed us the most." He forced long grass out of his way and they all trudged forward towards a red bumper line. As he was never comfortable talking about himself, he turned the conversation to her. "How are you and your son doing?"

"We're holding up. It's been easier with the others in the house."

"Yeah, that's kind of you. Glad to see I'm not the only one trying to help."

"Well, to be honest, I don't think I could stay in that

house by myself after what happened."

He nodded. "That night still baffles me."

"Yeah?" she asked glancing at him for a second then looking away.

"Three armed individuals and you took them all out."

"Don't come between a mother and her child, isn't that a saying?" Her lip curled.

Bands of sunshine shone through the trees lighting up the ground and creating shadows. The sound of the ocean crashing against the rocks, dominated.

"Look, I've been meaning to talk to you. I know I was a little hard on you when I brought you in for questioning but that was because until then we hadn't seen any real violence. And, my concern is for your son. To be blatantly honest, Sara, I don't care whether it was entirely you or someone else who helped you but if your son was involved, I'm worried about how it might affect him." She looked at him but didn't say anything. He had a sense from the beginning that Max was involved and she was just covering for him in case their actions led to some form of punishment. "How's he doing?"

She shrugged. "I would be lying to say he hasn't been affected but then again, I think telling him that his grandmother was dead shortly after hit him more than what he went through that night."

"I heard about that. I'm sorry for your loss."

"Thank you."

"Unfortunately your mother was one of many who died over the winter. It was brutal weather. I just hope we can be more prepared this coming year if this holds out," he said looking around.

Sara gave a nod. "You mind me asking what's happened to the department since this?"

He inhaled deeply. "It's running a skeleton crew throughout the county. No one is under obligation to work but a few have chosen to. For how long is anyone's guess."

"I've heard rumors that the government has imposed martial law and opened up FEMA camps in Bangor. You know anything about this?"

"Are you asking if it's happened or what would happen?"

"Both."

He nodded. "I heard the rumors too. As for what would happen, it's hard to know right now. We've never been in this position before but if the rumors are true, any number of things could happen. The U.S. Constitution would be suspended, as would civil rights, civil law and habeas corpus."

"Habeas what?"

He chuckled.

"In layman's terms it means the rights that protect a prisoner are removed. Basically the right to a fair trial is infringed upon."

"Like what Mick was trying to do today?"

"You heard about that?"

"Jake told me."

He nodded. "Yeah, except that Mick thinks he's above the law. He's about to find out he's not."

"But given enough time that could become the norm.

No judge, no jury, right?"

"Only if we let it." He blew his cheeks out. "Sara, you wanted to know why I'm still at this, it's because of that. People deserve a fair trial. If we leave the fate of people's lives in the hands of people like Mick, we will have anarchy."

"Don't we already have it?"

"Anarchy, no. At least not in these parts — chaos, panic, desperation, yeah."

"Sounds a lot like anarchy to me." She let out a small laugh.

Someone yelled, "I think I've found something." Sam was about to race over when the person picked up a soil-covered jacket. It looked as if it had been there for months. "False alert."

"Bag it," Sam said checking the ground to see if it had been disturbed.

"Oh my God. Nearly gave me a heart attack," Sara said. "Anyway, you were saying…?"

Sam continued. "Well, martial law could lead to no

freedom of press, no freedom of assembly, no freedom of speech, curfews enforced, troops in the streets to enforce these rules, checkpoints set up, and—"

"We already have checkpoints."

"Those were ours. Uh..." He trailed off not wanting to get into it. "Anyway, where was I?"

"Checkpoints."

"Right. The government could hold a person without charge, potentially arrest anyone who they think is a suspect of a crime, someone could be thrown in jail without representation or due process, and the worst of all… confiscation of firearms, ammunition and supplies."

"Worst of all? As if you can pick one thing that would be worse than another. It's all bad news."

He stifled a laugh. "You're right there. Essentially you lose all of your rights. Now for some they could see this as a good thing. I heard there were people who left Castine, heading for Bangor, who were more than willing to fall under those rules."

"But why?"

"Look around you, Sara. This isn't the land of the free. It never has been. Oh, we sing about it and celebrate it on the Fourth of July but the government has been and always will be there pulling the strings. It's a false sense of freedom."

"You don't believe in freedom?"

"I believe in it; I just don't think America has ever had it. Well, maybe at one time before all the laws and rules and regulations tightened the noose around our necks."

She found that amusing.

"What?" he asked.

"Well you work for the government. You're a civil servant. In a nutshell… the government's bitch."

He burst out laughing and she joined in. "Thanks for reminding me. I never thought of it that way."

"You're welcome."

Right then Carl came over the radio. "Sam. You find anything?"

"Only your date from the other night," he replied in jest.

"What?"

"Nothing. What about you?"

"We did come across a burnt-out vehicle. Which makes me wonder. Why not just kill the women in their homes, take what they needed and leave them be? Why leave them out in the open?"

"He wants them to be found."

"He?"

"Look, it seems pretty obvious, don't you think?"

"You think it's him, don't you?"

"Look at his track record, Carl. If anyone is capable, it's him. And with the power going out, this was just the opportunity he wanted."

"And if it's not?"

"Then we keep looking."

"Only one problem there, Sammy boy," Carl said. "Without a coroner to perform an autopsy, DNA, etc., we are grasping for straws. What we need is a witness. Someone that could pin him at the home of one of the women on the night she went missing."

"Trust me, buddy, I get it. That's what pisses me off," he said in a low voice. He didn't want everyone to know. "All right. Keep me updated if you find anything."

Sara immediately interjected. "You would probably have better luck setting him up."

"What do you mean?"

"The three who attacked us waited until we were alone. Sometimes that's what it takes to draw them out."

"You think we should lure out whoever is doing this? Make them a target?"

"You said you need a witness. The problem is, deputy, if whoever is behind this strikes again, you aren't going to know until it's already done. All three of these women were single and lived alone."

"And?"

"Whoever is doing this is watching, waiting for the right time to strike. Now my father said that if you want to catch a fish you have to use the right bait, at the right time in the right place. A single woman is your bait. You just need to make the bait alluring."

He couldn't believe he was listening to her idea or that she was seriously suggesting they put a woman's life in harm's way, but the fact was every woman that was living by herself was in harm's way. At least if they could focus the attention on one, they could potentially lure them out.

"Tell me more."

"Hold a community meeting. Announce that additional supplies have come into town and will be kept at the home of... Teresa, for instance. She's single. The town manager. People will buy it. They would expect her to be overseeing the distribution of supplies."

He snorted. "You want to put a crosshair on Teresa?"

"Can you think of anyone better?"

"No but she will go ballistic when I suggest this."

"Putting surveillance on one home versus trying to watch every home would make your job a lot easier. And you never know, you might just catch a murderer."

He laughed. "You should consider becoming a cop."

Sara smiled and kicked out some loose stones from the

earth. "I did at one time but decided to take over the Manor."

"Huh. You might have made a good one." He nodded, contemplating whether it would work or not. He'd have to get the idea by Teresa and that woman was a nightmare at the best of times. "I will give it some thought."

They continued searching for several hours, only stopping to drink and have something to eat. The sun was beginning to wane behind the trees and they'd only covered a fraction of the woods. It seemed like an impossible task. He was beginning to think they wouldn't find Debbie and she'd turn up a few days later with some story about leaving town for some abnormal reason.

That thought went out of his mind when a red flare shot up into the sky, and Jake came over the radio. "Sam. We've found her not far from Trask Rock."

"You sure it's her?"

"That's her. I remember towing her car one winter."

Sam motioned to the others and they all broke into a

jog heading for the west side. Trask Rock was a mammoth rock considered the world's largest pebble as it was located on a pebbly beach. As they hurried, Sam turned to Sara. "Your idea. I'll run it by Teresa. I hate to admit it but it might be the only way we catch this asshole."

As they made their way down the shore, Sam's stomach caught in his throat at the thought of finding another body. If Mick was behind this, he was leaving them out in the open almost in a taunting fashion. If it was him, he would make damn sure he paid.

Chapter 22

Landon should have been angry but strangely he wasn't. Perhaps it was because he was too tired to care, or he'd come to realize that life was in the habit of sending curveballs, and maybe this was payback for those they'd killed — like some twisted form of karma. Sara was always saying that whatever you did came back to you tenfold. Something to do with the law of attraction, vibrations and whatnot. He was starting to believe it was true. So yeah, he should have been pissed but he wasn't.

Beth on the other hand was fuming. She'd flipped the picnic table, kicked a garbage can over and screamed like a banshee before dropping to her knees, exhausted. He just let her blow off steam, waiting for when she had nothing left in her. He could have told her to pull her shit together but it was to be expected; she was sleep deprived, still grieving the loss of her father and had gone through the worst two days.

"I'm going after them," she said scooping up her rifle and slinging it over her shoulder. Landon was quick to put a stop to that, rising to his feet and getting in front of her.

"Don't be stupid, Beth. That was two hours ago. They'd be long gone by now and there is no telling which way they went. I don't expect they headed for Damascus."

She stabbed a finger at the trail ahead of them. "You don't get it, do you? Hiking the AT is hard enough with supplies but take that away and we are screwed."

"We still have one sleeping bag, a bivy, rifles, handguns and some ammo."

"Oh wonderful," she said sarcastically. "I feel so much better!"

"Really?"

"No! We have no water bottles, no means of purifying, no food, no means of staying warm or dry, no stove, no…" She rattled on listing every item down to the very last thing as if that would somehow solidify in his mind the weight of it all. He wasn't stupid, he understood the gravity, but in comparison to losing Ellie, their problems paled.

In his mind he was living on borrowed time.

"You done ranting?" he asked.

"Oh fuck you, Landon. If it wasn't for you, I wouldn't even be here!"

He nodded, and studied her with a steadfast expression. "No, you're probably right."

She continued, tiredness getting the better of her. It was all bubbling to the surface and in some ways he was glad. Experience had taught him that bottling up deep-seated emotion wasn't healthy. She put on this brave front but below it all she was just an eighteen-year-old girl that had been thrown into the worst possible situation. She'd known more grief in her short life than he ever had. It was for those reasons and more he didn't take her words to heart.

"Get it out. You have a right to be angry but it doesn't change our situation."

"That's right. It doesn't. But I'm gonna find them

and…"

"They're gone, Beth. Just like your father, just like Ellie and just like the world we once knew."

She stopped ranting and looked at him, then perched on the edge of the shelter and placed her hands on her knees as she lowered her chin. "There are hundreds of towns out there that we can scavenge for supplies. Hell, we might get lucky and find someone with a heart," he said.

"What, like Terry and Nancy?"

Silence stretched between them as he sat beside her.

He patted her on the leg. "Get some sleep, we'll deal with this later."

"It will be too late by then. It'll be dark. Cold. And…"

"We'll survive," he said placing a hand on her shoulder. "Look at all the shit we've been through so far. And we're still here. That's because you're strong, and stubborn." She glanced at him and that got a strained smile out of her. "And your father taught you well. Think about what he would have done," Landon said rising to his feet and stretching. He could have easily slept another few hours but she was right, it would soon be dark and they would need food. He planned on heading into the woods and seeing if he could bag himself a rabbit but before he did that, he went over to Grizzly to make sure he was okay. He dropped down and ran a hand through his hair. Grizzly lifted his eyelid but closed it again.

"They drugged him," Beth said, getting this bitter look on her face. He knew she would have gone after them but anger could cloud judgment and that was all they had going for them right now. Make good choices, he told himself.

"Where you going?" she asked.

"To find dinner."

She snorted. "You ever caught anything?"

"No, but I guess I better learn fast, right?" he said turning around and grinning. In all truth he was wearing his own mask. Inwardly he was freaking out.

"Hold up, I'll come help."

"Beth. I can do it. Just get some rest. I think after

we've had something to eat, we should press on through the night."

She didn't argue. Tiredness had got the better of her. He watched her climb into the sleeping bag, taking her rifle in with her. He knew she would be sleeping with one eye open, that's why he had no qualms about leaving the campsite. Besides, he wasn't planning on straying too far.

Once he was out of sight, he pressed his back up against a tree and dropped down to a crouch. He rubbed the bridge of his nose, feeling the full weight of the situation. He couldn't let her see it, it would only fuel her reason for trying to track Terry and Nancy. "Okay, you can do this." He brought up his rifle and scanned the terrain. He'd never hunted in his life. One of his close friends lived for this kind of stuff and had invited him out a few times but he'd never bothered. Something about being eaten alive by mosquitoes and waiting around in a tree stand just didn't appeal to him. He had no problem with those who loved it but it just wasn't his thing. Now he wished he'd taken him up on that offer. The only skill he possessed was flying planes, and firing guns at the range.

Was he meant to go high? Or just wait in the brush for one to come along? Ugh, he had no idea. Landon spent the better part of an hour changing up his approach until he settled on staying still and hoping to God something came along.

Chapter 23

Ruby severed the man's head, and lifted it triumphantly.

His companion screamed; her voice echoed in the valley. Still dripping blood, Ruby rose from the ground and carried it over to the female who was forced to witness the horrendous death. Eve and Trinity had kept a firm grip on her as she tried to escape. Ruby shoved the head in her face. "Come on, darlin', give him a kiss," she said with a smile on her face while trying to force the decapitated head's lips against the woman.

They'd encountered the two hikers not far from Taylors Valley while searching for Beth and Landon. All she knew was the little Lilith had told her prior to her death; that they were heading for Maine and planned on going via the Appalachian Trail. She assumed they would stop in Damascus but no one had seen two travelers matching their description. She could have dropped it, let them go on their way but with being second in line to Lilith, what kind of message would that send to the other girls? No, she was determined to make them pay for what they'd done. She and two others had joined the Appalachian Trail with the hope of finding them camping a few miles in.

Eve believed they were wasting their time, and after trekking so many miles through the worst weather, Ruby was beginning to think she was right until they happened to cross paths with the two hikers.

Call it fate.

Call it luck.

She didn't give a shit what people thought, it was perfect timing. Had they not found them within a few more hours she was ready to turn back.

Had the hikers not been carrying their backpacks they might have just passed them with nothing more than a hello, and a nod of the head. But Ruby remembered the unique leather bag with the small North Carolina badge attached to it, and a colorful red and green bandanna tied off around the strap. It was Beth's, of that she was sure. And there was no way in hell she would have given that up unless forced.

Her mind flashed back to minutes earlier while his companion screamed.

Ruby had walked by the man and looked back. "Excuse me. I couldn't help but notice the North Carolina badge. Are you both from there?"

The man gave a nervous glance to his female companion then nodded. "That's right. We're hiking back. Came all the way from Maine."

"Maine?" Ruby asked.

He nodded. "Is that where you're heading?"

"Possibly." Ruby approached the man while Eve and Trinity circled them to ensure they didn't run. "You wouldn't by any chance have some spare water, would you?"

"Yeah, but we don't have a lot. There is a stream about a mile up from here. Shouldn't take you too long," the man said.

"Pity. I'm real thirsty."

"Sorry. It's just we need to get going. It will be dark soon and…"

"You in a hurry?" Ruby asked, resting her hand on the handgun around her waist. She'd already noticed they weren't packing. That was the first mistake they made, the second was crossing paths with them, and the third was him denying her request. The man nudged his companion and bid them farewell before turning to leave. They hadn't made it more than four feet when she pulled her revolver and cocked it.

Both of them froze.

His female companion's hands went up but his didn't.

"Look, you want what we have, take it. It's just…"

There was nothing that riled her more than a man who thought he could talk his way out of a bad situation. Before he could finish, she ripped the bag from his shoulders and rifled through it, pulling out items that only a female would use, someone who had periods. One glance at the woman and she was certain she was out of that stage.

"This yours?" she said bringing out a few female hygiene products.

"We found them, several miles from here."

"Really? Where?"

"Near a river. We figured the owners had gone for a swim or left them behind."

Ruby laughed as she rose. "Gone for a swim. Left behind." She snorted. "Do I look like I'm stupid?" she asked tapping the revolver against her leg.

"No."

"Where did you get them?"

"I told you, we—"

Before he was done, she fired a round into his leg causing him to drop to the ground, rolling around in agony. "Don't bullshit me," Ruby said sliding the revolver back into her holster and pulling out a serrated blade that she'd used a number of times on men with an attitude who'd wandered into their neck of the woods. She pointed the tip of the knife at him. "I'm going to make this really easy for you. I know the owner of this bag. A young girl, with dirty blond hair, and the other one belongs to a middle-aged man. So how about you answer the question again. Where did you get these?"

He swallowed hard. "We stole them. Satisfied? We're just trying to survive. Just like anyone else."

"Hey, a man's got to do what a man's got to do, isn't that right?"

The guy nodded, his hands gripping his bloody leg.

"So were the girl and guy around when you stole them?"

"Asleep."

"Asleep. Oh perfect. So you just waltzed in there and took it from underneath their nose." Ruby started clapping her hands "Bravo. That takes some real balls."

"We didn't hurt them, if they're friends of yours."

What a pussy, she thought.

"That's good. Because that would have really taken the fun out of what we had planned." The man stopped grimacing and frowned. Ruby got close to him and jabbed the knife near the wound on his leg. The man covered it with both hands. "Where are they?"

"Lost Mountain Shelter. It's about eight and a half miles from here. Stay on this trail and you'll see signs for it." She stared him in the eyes. Was he telling the truth? There was only one way to find out. She walked around the back of him and then in an instant dropped down and brought the blade up to his neck.

"No, please. Please. I've told you what you wanted to know."

"But I can't be sure you're telling me the truth," Ruby said.

The female companion was quick to interject. "He is. We haven't lied. We stole the backpacks. They are at the shelter. Please. We beg you. Take everything we have. Just let us go."

Ruby bit down on her lower lip, studying the woman's face. She smiled and for a second the female companion thought she would change her mind but she hadn't.

"Only one problem with that."

"What?"

"I asked you for water and you denied my request. And one glance in the bag and it's clear you had plenty of water. Once a liar, always a liar." With that said she slid the razor-sharp blade across the man's throat, cutting him from ear to ear. In a fit of rage she decapitated him and raised his head, feeling vindicated for every time a man had wronged her.

Ruby ran her bloody hand around the woman's face and spoke in a soft voice. "Hey. Hey. Don't you worry. We're not gonna hurt you," Ruby said before squeezing her cheeks. "You're one of us. Now go. Go on. On your way," she said, gesturing to Eve and Trinity to release her. The woman looked hesitant at first as if she didn't believe they would let her go but Ruby was a woman of her word. Ruby gave her a shove. "Go on. Move it now before I change my mind." They let her carry her own bag but kept Beth and Landon's bags. They watched as the woman ran away from them not looking back for even a second.

Eve laughed. "I gotta say, Ruby, even for you that was cold."

"He got what he deserved."

Trinity sidled up to Ruby. "What do you want to do with the bags?"

"Dump them. They won't be needing them."

They took out the essentials such as water and food but the rest was tossed into the forest. Once done, they took off heading for Lost Mountain Shelter.

Chapter 24

"Out of the question!" Teresa bellowed, as Sam followed her down the corridor into her office. "You want to put me in harm's way? Deputy, are you out of your mind?" She looked as if she was about to blow a gasket. Carl and Jake had tagged along for moral support. Carl closed the door behind them as Teresa went around her desk and shot him dagger eyes. Sam didn't expect it would be an easy sell being that Teresa would be the target. "If it wasn't for the fact that society has collapsed, I would report you to your chief."

"Wouldn't do much, he'd probably find it funny," Carl said.

That only infuriated her more. Sam nudged him. He wasn't helping.

"Look, Teresa. I understand the hesitation."

"Hesitation?! That would imply I was considering it. I'm not. No one in their right mind would go through with this." He glanced at his watch. They were an hour away from the town hall meeting that occurred every week to keep the community updated on the situation. They didn't have long to convince her.

"What I meant to say was that I understand you don't want to do it, but think about it. We are chasing a ghost. We have no suspect description, no name, nothing to go on. This person or persons will continue to do this unless we think outside the box."

"Oh, this is outside the box, all right."

Sam sighed and ran a hand around the back of his sweaty neck. He was tired, his legs ached from searching for the third woman, and he was in no mood to deal with her. Sure, it was dangerous but not any more than doing nothing.

"The approach we are taking isn't working. We have to reevaluate and adapt to our circumstances. And right now those are not good. How many more women need to die, Teresa, before you take this seriously?"

"Watch your tone."

Sam shot Carl a glance. Carl had this grin on his face. All he needed now was a box of popcorn and he would be in his element.

"Look, I know you enjoy running this town from your ivory tower but people are dying out there. And hey, you would think that's the worst of it, but it's not." She gave him a look of confusion. "It's dealing with men like Mick that is going to turn this town against you, me and what little order is left. Right now he wants us to fail because that would prove him right. It would fuel the flames and push the rest of the community over the edge to side with him. And you saw what nearly happened out there. An innocent man was almost hung."

"Innocent? You don't know that."

"Innocent until proven guilty," Sam replied.

She narrowed her eyes at him. "Which reminds me. Have you followed up? What if Mick is right? What if he did rape this girl? Have you even spoken to her?"

"If that's the case, he will be tried. For the time being he's being held in Ellsworth."

"Tried." She laughed. "I think you're missing something, deputy. We don't have a judge, hell we don't even have a local jail besides the one in Ellsworth and I expect that's full by now. Am I right?"

He glanced at Carl. She wasn't far wrong. Four months without power had led to a rise in criminal activity, all of which meant the limited number of cells were now being shared by multiple prisoners. Instead of answering he kept the conversation on point.

"Look, will you do it or not?"

"No. I just told you."

"You mind…" Jake piped up. He looked at both of them. Sam was done trying to convince her. He made a gesture to Jake and he rose from his seat. "Teresa. If someone asked me to do it, I would probably say no as well. I value my life without a doubt. However, after what I saw Sara go through, I can't imagine what those three women endured or what other women will suffer through if we don't catch this animal fast. What if someone was in the house with you?"

That caught everyone's attention. The original plan was they would be stationed outside in various positions watching the home through binoculars. At the first sign of trouble they would move in.

"I'm listening," she said.

"Any of us could be in there with you. That way if anything happened, we can intervene fast. If this person or group is following the same pattern, they would attempt to take you out of the home."

She scowled at Sam. "And you still haven't answered why they did that?"

"Isn't it obvious?" Carl interjected. He didn't need to spell it out but they believed the victims were sexually assaulted before they were murdered. It also fed into Sam's theory that Mick was behind it as his home wasn't far from Witherle Woods. Based on the wound to the back of the head of each victim, and grazes on the heels of two of the women, he made an assumption that all three victims had been struck on the head from behind, dragged out of the house and taken somewhere else. He didn't think they were killed in the forest but that was where they were dumped. Of course an autopsy would have to determine that but that wasn't going to happen.

Teresa shook her head. "I don't know. If I was to agree I wouldn't want either of these two in the house, that's for sure." She turned up her nose while pointing at Sam and Carl. It was to be expected. He rubbed her up the wrong way, and likewise.

"That's fine," Sam said. "Jake, would you go with her?"

"Would be my pleasure."

"There, that's settled."

"Hold on a minute. I didn't say I agreed to it. I said I would consider it." She lifted her nose and walked over to the window in her office and looked out. "And you would be armed, I presume, Jake?"

"I would."

"Very well, it's settled," she said spinning around. Sam rolled his eyes. She was going to agree anyway but she just wanted to be the one to say it was settled. Honestly, he didn't give two craps as long as he managed to get his hands on Mick. He turned to leave when Teresa continued. "Deputy. I'm not done." Oh she was really throwing her weight around now. He could see the smug look on her face as he turned to face her.

"I know you want to believe that Mick Bennington is behind this but what if he's not? At some point we are going to have to make some hard decisions on what to do with those who break the law. Maybe Mick went about it the wrong way but he has a point."

"Oh please. Don't tell me he's got in your head now."

She came around the table, lips pursed, her hands clasped together behind her back. "Your history with Mick, deputy, is just that — it's history. I don't want it getting in the way of what we are trying to do here."

"And what would that be, Teresa?"

She smiled and leaned in to speak into his ear so the other two couldn't hear her. "Don't be smart with me. You might regret it," she said. If he wasn't mistaken that sounded like a threat. But who the hell was she to threaten anyone? Her power over this town ended the day the lights went out, at least that's what he figured. She backed off and answered his question.

"To keep the peace and protect people, what do you think? Dear me, deputy, maybe someone needs to go back to police college," she said before returning to her leather throne behind her desk. Sam ground his teeth and exited the room.

"See you at the meeting, deputy," Teresa said in a mocking tone.

He so badly wanted to turn around and toss her the bird but instead he refrained.

Chapter 25

It was the perfect shot. Landon's jaw dropped in surprise. He couldn't believe his eyes. He'd done it. Nailed his first rabbit. He bounced on the balls of his feet from behind the boulder and did a little jig. If Sara could see him now. It was the closest he'd felt to nature. Okay, it had taken him several hours but still, a kill was a kill.

Landon hurried over to collect his prize.

Now if Beth could just work her magic and start a fire, like the way she'd shown him she could without matches, they would be in business. He lifted the furry animal by the back legs. "Sorry, my friend, but we've gotta eat."

It was at that point he turned and realized that he didn't know where he was. His stomach sank as he turned a full 360 degrees. At first he'd kept the camp in sight and only ventured a short way from the path but getting no luck he'd pressed farther in. *Damn it. I should have used chalk or string to mark the trees.* It was a rookie mistake.

He was so consumed with finding something to eat, it didn't cross his mind that he was getting farther away from the campsite.

"Beth!" he bellowed a few times.

Okay, don't panic. You got this. Hell, you just proved you can nab a rabbit. Now what was it she said about the sun, which incidentally had all but disappeared behind the trees? He tried to remember what Beth had told him about using the sun to determine north, east, south and west. It was something to do with times of the day. *Damn it.* He had a memory like a sieve. *Why can't you remember?* He'd always been like that. Remembering the small insignificant things and forgetting the stuff that really mattered. It certainly had presented a lot of problems when he was learning to fly.

"Beth!"

He knew the first rule about getting lost in the woods was to stay put but darkness was creeping in and there was no way in hell he was getting stuck out there. It had been hard enough in the day. "Well you came from that way," he said noting how the tall grass had been pressed down. He began trudging back hoping to God he was on the right path. Every few minutes he would call out her name.

* * *

Beth squirmed within her grasp hearing the distant sound of Landon's voice. She could smell the blood on her hands. Ruby whispered in her ear. "Now, now, let's not give away the big surprise." A knife jabbed her in the ribs causing her to flinch.

She wasn't sleeping when they ambushed her nor was her weapon out of reach, in fact she'd managed to pull it when they emerged from the tree line, rifles raised at her.

Her dog was still sedated but slowly coming out of it.

Even if she'd managed to kill one of them, the other two would have taken her out.

"Alert him and you die," Ruby had said before they'd hurried in and disarmed her.

At first Beth tried to cover for Landon by saying they'd parted ways but Ruby didn't buy it. That's when she told her about striking up a conversation with two hikers on the way in. Then she proceeded to tell her the grisly details of how she decapitated him as if finding joy in her reaction.

Ruby and the two women had dragged Beth behind the shelter into a large patch of tall grass, waiting for Landon to emerge. "I have to admit you two pulled off what few achieved. You know, there were many others like you. Hunters. A group from a town over who thought they could take back Mountain City but no one managed to do it. Now I know you didn't do it all by yourself, you had help from Robbie." She sighed as if she cared. Then a flicker of a smile formed. "Lilith had such high hopes for him. Such a waste." She shook her head. "Oh I completely forgot to tell you what happened. You didn't stick around to see the grand finale." Ruby let go of Beth's face. She'd turned it so she could look at her. "I shot him in the head."

Beth balled her hands and Ruby saw it. She pressed the knife harder against her rib cage. "Don't even think about it."

Right then they heard Landon getting closer. "Showtime!" Ruby said.

Once again, Landon was pleased with himself. Maybe this survival stuff wasn't as hard as it looked, he thought as he saw the campsite between the trees and called out to Beth. When he didn't get a response, he slowed.

Raising his rifle, he squinted and moved slowly between the pine trees trying to get a better look at the front of the shelter. He saw the bivy was zipped up but couldn't tell if she was inside. Grizzly was still where he last saw him though his head was up and looking off towards the far side of the shelter. Landon followed his gaze. "What are you looking at?" He said to himself

That's when he saw it. Movement. It was ever so slight but enough that it caught his eye. A smidgen of color that looked out of place among the rippling waves of green. Then a face, female, older than Beth. His gaze darted to Grizzly then back again. Had they seen him? He backed away, moving slowly to the cover of a tree, and then checked how many rounds he had. Besides the shootout in the cabin, he'd never killed anyone. His pulse sped up, and his mouth went dry. Landon knew the moment he entered that camp he would be ambushed, and yet if he fired upon them there was a chance they could kill Beth, if they hadn't already. *Okay, breathe. Breathe. You can do this.*

How many were there?

His imagination played havoc on his mind as he recalled the Neva Grill.

What if he was outnumbered? He snuck another peek around the tree, his stomach catching in his throat. What if he waited them out? No, they'd heard him calling. It wouldn't take long before they realized he'd seen them.

He brought up the rifle and peered through the scope. What kind of distance could this thing get? How far out were they? If he fired a round and it missed that wouldn't be good for her or him. Staying low he shifted from one tree to the next trying to get a better view of who he was dealing with. His mind told him Ruby but it could be anyone. For all he knew it could be the two hikers, returned with others.

Think. Think fast.

He adjusted the scope and he saw her beside Beth, knife pressed into her side. No. A slight level adjustment and he got her temple in the crosshair. Just as Landon was bringing his finger to the trigger, Ruby moved.

There was a loud screeching cry, followed by a commotion.

Bringing the scope to his eye he swept the rifle from side to side until he saw the hiker — Nancy — holding a boulder in her hand the size of a basketball. She was slamming it as hard as she could against something — no — someone below her. She had a wound to the gut but that wasn't slowing her down one bit. She brought down the boulder fast and furious.

Landon knew it was his moment.

They were distracted.

He burst forward, his pants swishing against the underbrush.

A round erupted. Followed by another crack, and then it was over.

Two remained. Ruby held on to Beth tightly while the second woman, with short ginger hair, lowered her rifle. Landon dropped to a knee and brought his rifle up. Seconds. That's all he had before they dropped down into the cover of the tall grass. He brought the rifle up and got the ginger bitch in his crosshair.

Slow it down.

Breathe out.

Steady.

Crack!

He squeezed the trigger and a round punctured the woman's skull, taking her down in a red mist. Ruby dropped and began yelling. "I will kill her. I will slice her from ear to ear. You hear me?"

He didn't respond.

Landon was already two steps ahead.

After taking the shot he darted from one tree to the next to see if he could get into a better location, one that would give him a clear shot. Ruby was frantic. Her head dipped behind Beth, using her as a shield as she continued to shout.

Then she pulled her back, retreating towards the thicket of trees.

Landon knew if she made it in there, he would have little to no chance of catching her. It was dense, overgrown and unlike the clearing that only had tall grass, there were plenty of places to take cover.

C'mon, Beth. C'mon!

As if reading his mind, Beth reacted with an elbow to her gut and then blasted away from her. Ruby lifted the knife to throw it and Landon released a round while saying a silent prayer under his breath.

The round struck her square in the chest, knocking Ruby down.

Not wasting a second, he rushed in, not even stopping to check Beth.

There among the grass he found Ruby gurgling, and suffocating on her own blood.

Her eyes were wide as she looked at him. It looked as if she was trying to say something but just as her lips tried to form the word, she breathed her last.

Landon scanned for more threats.

"Any more, Beth?" he asked without looking at her.

"That's it," she replied. Landon turned and Beth rushed toward him.

For a second the exchange was awkward as if he didn't know what to do but then his arm wrapped around her and he squeezed her tight. As he held her, he looked over at Nancy. Nearby was another woman, her skull smashed in with the boulder Nancy had used. Had it not been for her returning, maybe it would have played out very differently.

Chapter 26

Sam could sense trouble brewing the moment he arrived for the meeting. Crowds had gathered outside. Most carried signs that declared their rights. He squeezed through the mob; a few angry gazes shot his way. It was the largest turnout they'd had since the lights had gone out. There were those who had genuine concerns, others just looking to rant, and the rest were there to support Mick. His group of thirty or more huddled together on one side of the cramped school auditorium. The hall had been divided into two sides with twenty rows of chairs on either side.

As soon as Mick saw him, he gave this smug grin.

Oh, he was looking to start something.

He knew they would bombard them with questions about the missing women, and what had become of the man taken into custody. Mick would try to rile up the crowd and incite an outburst, that's why Sam had Jake contact ten of the people who had helped with the search today to get them to act as security. He left it for Jake to decide which ten would be best suited. At this point he knew he had to rely on others and so far, Jake hadn't let him down.

A solar generator had been brought in to power a microphone that was wired into two amps on each side of the room. Teresa stepped up to the microphone and gave it a short tap. "Testing." It let out a squeal. Several people put their fingers in their ears and ground their teeth at the high-pitched sound. Rodney Jennings, the local university whiz kid, was in charge of the system and was quick to adjust the volume.

"I appreciate all of you coming out this evening. Now —"

"Where is he!" Mick bellowed, cutting her off.

"Please. Quiet down. There will be a time to ask your questions but we have a lot to cover this evening."

"I knew it. I knew you wouldn't do anything. Let me guess, he's back out on the streets. Is that right?"

"You heard what she said, Mick. Now quiet down or leave," Sam shouted from across the auditorium.

"Or what? What you gonna do?"

"You'll be removed."

"By you?"

Sam pointed to those assisting that evening. Mick glanced at a couple and snorted.

He whispered something into the ear of the man beside him. The man flashed a grin before squeezing his way out of the building. With a nod of the head, Carl followed to make sure he wasn't going to cause trouble.

Teresa continued. "First things first, we have had a new supply of food come into town, donated from a nearby town. All supplies will be taken to my residence tonight after the meeting and will remain there until we determine how they will be distributed to those in need. As mentioned in our previous meeting, anyone wishing to put in a request for items must fill out one of the forms at the back of the room. We will take each request on a case-by-case basis. As it stands, children, the elderly and those in care will be receiving the focus of our attention. All that remains after that will be rationed out to the rest of you." She put her glasses on and looked down a sheet of paperwork in front of her. "Now as you know, rumors have been circulating about martial law being in effect and FEMA camps. I can confirm that there is a camp in operation in Bangor but as for when and if we will fall under the oversight of military, that will be determined this coming week when I speak to a worker from FEMA."

Sam looked at her and Teresa's lip went up.

She'd held back those cards. When was she planning on telling him that?

That was information he would have liked to know, information that could affect the decisions, and supplies they had.

"Are the military coming to Castine?" a woman asked.

"At this time I cannot answer that. We are still dealing with a lot of unknowns."

Sam turned his head towards the main door and saw Carl reappear. He raised a hand and made a gesture which made it look like it was urgent. Sam went to leave and Teresa turned to him, placing a hand over the microphone. "Where are you going?"

"I'll be right back." He made his way around the room, squeezing past several people until he reached Carl. "What is it?"

"You need to see this."

He didn't like the sound of that. Carl hurried out of the building with Sam in his shadow. As soon as they emerged, his eyes widened. "What the hell!" The Toyota Land Cruiser they'd been using was a blazing inferno. Flames licked up into the night sky. Any chance of saving it was gone. "That bastard! This was him."

"Sam. No. Wait," Carl said.

Before he could stop him, Sam charged back into the meeting and made a beeline for Mick. Mick saw him at the last second, just as he plowed into him, knocking him back into a woman and causing her to scream. Heads turned; all eyes were on them as he slammed him up against the wall. "What is it, deputy? What I have done?"

he said with a smirk on his face.

"You know damn well! You are under arrest."

"For what?"

Several of Mick's closest fishing buddies tried to get Sam off him but he shoved them back and then pulled his service weapon.

"Deputy Daniels! That's enough!" Teresa bellowed elbowing her way through the throng of people. "Put that away now and tell me what is going on."

"This asshole is what's going on. He set our vehicle on fire."

"How? I was here all the time."

"It was one of your men."

Sam still hadn't taken his one hand off Mick's shirt. He kept him pressed against the wall.

"Sam. Sam!" Carl said. "It wasn't him."

"What?"

"That's what I was trying to tell you but you wouldn't listen. We've caught the guy, in fact Mick's pal caught him trying to run. Right then Niles, the same man who'd left a few minutes before, returned with another one of Mick's buddies, pushing a guy into the room."

"Let him go," Teresa said to Sam. He stood there for a second not moving as if his brain was trying to comprehend it. Every part of him wanted to believe it was Mick. Their history, what about their history? Sam released his grip on Mick's shirt and backed up without saying a word. He slipped his gun into the holster and approached Carl.

"Are you sure?"

"Positive. I saw him do it myself," Carl said.

"You have something to say, deputy?" Mick said, reveling in the public humiliation. He looked at Mick and nodded slowly. Somehow, he was behind this. He was sure of that. He'd done this to make a mockery of him, to make the community doubt his ability just as he had the day he announced in front of the hall that he hadn't done anything to bring closure to the missing women situation.

Sam approached the man who'd set the vehicle ablaze.

"Why? Why did you do it?"

The man didn't give him an answer.

Without giving an apology to Mick he turned and walked out leaving Carl to deal with the onslaught of questions.

Chapter 27

The tumultuous evening abruptly came to a head at the end of Mayo Point Road, at the residence of Teresa McKenna. After a raging argument following the meeting, Sam was more than willing to walk but instead he put her in her place by telling her that if she wanted to shit on the department and report him, and tell them what to do when they weren't getting paid, go ahead, but she'd better be ready to take responsibility for the deaths of Castine residents when the lights came back on.

That certainly made her pause for thought.

Obviously, they weren't coming on anytime soon but she didn't know that and it was just the motivation she needed to go through with the evening's plan.

"You really think this is gonna work?" Carl asked over the radio as he crouched in the surrounding woodland with a rifle in hand. Carl was positioned in the tree line near the waterfront side. Unfortunately for Jake, he was inside with Teresa. Her two-story contemporary home was located on the river and provided breathtaking views of the Bagaduce.

Another reason why it was an ideal location for what they had in mind was because it could only be reached by heading down a quiet private road or by boat. There was one way in and out. On the east side was the river, on the west a dense woodland. Sam had positioned himself on the west with a clear shot of the front of the home.

In order to keep it a secret, they were the only ones besides Teresa that knew about the evening's plan. They had considered bringing in another five residents to help but there was no way of knowing if word would get out and whoever was behind the killings wouldn't show. The truth was there was no telling if they would anyway.

The whole plan was a shot in the dark.

"Why, you got your doubts?" Sam asked.

"It depends if whoever was doing this was at the meeting tonight. If they weren't, they'll be a no show."

"If they are, we'll be doing this every night for a week.

Eventually word will get out. If supplies are truly the incentive, this is like hanging a carrot on a string in front of a mule."

"Is Teresa the carrot or the mule?" Carl said before chuckling.

That brought a smile to Sam's face.

"You know, Sam, about this evening."

"Drop it."

"No, I get it. I would have probably done the same thing. But what is the deal with him?"

Sam wasn't sure exactly when he first locked horns with Mick. It could be argued that it started after he tossed him out of a bar one too many times, or arrested him for driving under the influence, or exchanged fists when he was called out to his home on a domestic. All he knew was that they hadn't seen eye to eye since those times, and Mick had gone out of his way to put himself in situations that would draw police attention.

He was like a kid testing his boundaries and when confronted would declare he knew his rights and request a supervisor. It caused untold delays. Sam was all for people knowing their rights. He wasn't a fool. He knew that taxpayer dollars paid his wages but nothing pissed him off more than people wasting first responders' time. He could have gone to another call, but instead he found himself bumping heads with that loser.

Over the years Mick had gained one hell of a track record as a violent drunk and an abuser of women. If there was ever a suspect in this case, it had his name all over it.

"Look, just keep your eyes peeled. If anyone shows up tonight it will probably be more than one person."

"Don't worry, Jake is in there."

"He's the last resort. I don't want them reaching the house, otherwise I will never hear the end of it from the witch."

"So that's what you're calling her. Guess it makes a difference from the hog."

"The hog?" Sam laughed.

"Well she reminds me of a wild hog."

"Don't let her hear you say that."

"Ah, who cares. What she gonna do, fire me?"

Under the cover of darkness they waited there as a cold breeze blew in off the river. "Thank God it's not summer. I'd be eaten alive by mosquitoes by now," Carl said. "So what do you think of deputizing Jake?"

"I think he's a good candidate. Whether he's up for the task is another thing entirely."

Carl's chuckle came over the radio. "Seems ironic that a guy who gets people out of bad situations showed up at the right time and helped us out."

Sam was half listening; his eyes were scanning the road and his ears listening for a vehicle. "You know, whoever is doing this must have access to a vehicle to transport the women to Witherle Woods. If this doesn't work out, I think our next step is to take a census of all the owners of operational vehicles. I'm sure it won't take long."

"That relies on people telling the truth, Sam. I imagine there are some folks out there who have old bangers that are working but won't say a word out of fear of having them confiscated by yours truly."

He sighed and ran a hand over his tired face. "What did you make of Teresa's admission this evening?"

"About FEMA and the military?"

"Yeah."

"Kind of figured she'd hold back. She wants to be at the helm of this town. Probably thinks if she's the mouthpiece, there might be perks in it for her. You know, like extra rations and whatnot. I don't like her but she's a smart woman."

"Deceptive."

"Deceptive, smart, it's all the same."

He nodded slowly, squinting into the darkness.

"What about the girl? Casey Wilmington."

"I sent Pete Hodges and Vera around to speak with her. Take her statement and go from there."

"You sent civilians to do it?"

"Carl. I'm juggling a lot of plates. Pete and Vera are caring folk. They have counseling experience. There really isn't much to getting a statement. I told them the questions to ask."

"But still."

"Hey, if we weren't out here now, I would go do it myself."

"You don't believe him, do you? Mick, I mean."

Sam didn't reply.

"What if he's right? What if that guy did sexually assault her?"

"He'll be dealt with."

"Uh-huh," Carl replied. Sam shook his head; he really didn't want to get into it. The conversation died and he was glad for the silence. Seconds turned into minutes, minutes into an hour with nothing happening.

Sam got back on the radio. "Carl, anything?"

Carl never replied.

"Carl. Come in, over."

Again nothing.

"Ah man, you better not be sleeping on the job."

It wasn't uncommon to find cops snoozing away the hours inside their cruisers, parked behind some store in a large parking lot, but now? Of all times. Sam tried getting through to him a few more times but got no answer. Eventually, he got up and jogged across Mayo Point Road around the back of the house down towards the boathouse. "Carl," Sam said in a low voice. "Hey." As he got closer to where he'd left him, he saw him lying down. "Oh man, for goodness' sakes. Of all the nights to sleep on the job." He hurried over and loomed over him, giving him a quick kick. "Hey, get up."

He didn't move.

"Carl?"

Sam dropped down and noticed blood trickling down the side of his face. He placed two fingers on his aorta. He was still breathing. Sam took out his flashlight and shone it on his face. Someone had cracked him on top of the head, and knocked him unconscious. "Carl. Carl!" he hollered shaking him but he only let out a murmur. "Shit! Hang tight, buddy." Sam lifted his rifle and took off at a sprint towards the house.

Chapter 28

It was stuffy in that pantry closet. Jake couldn't believe he'd agreed to her request. Even though Sam wanted her in the living room where he could see her silhouette through the blinds, Teresa refused. She wanted to be in her kitchen. He wasn't sure if that was true or if she just didn't like taking orders from Sam. He assumed it was a bit of both. No, according to her, if she was going to be waiting all night for some intruder, she at least wanted to stay busy and preferably in a place where she had access to a large kitchen knife.

Through the slats in the door he could see a countertop loaded with mason jars full of pickle juice. Propped up against the backsplash of her wall was a Rachael Ray cookbook. A solar generator churned away in the background, providing her with enough power to light the kitchen. Teresa was wearing a black apron over a long-sleeved white shirt with black pants and flats. She hummed as she chopped up cucumbers, carrots, cauliflower, beets, you name it, she planned on pickling it all. It was like a pickle fiesta, and she was in the running to win the award for the most pickled vegetables.

Cramped; Jake groaned as he twisted his body and moved his head from side to side. The pantry was overloaded with enough food to feed multiple families. She'd told him that no one was to know about it. He thought it was the supplies that had been gifted to the community but he came to learn that was nothing but a ruse. Now he wondered how she managed to have so many supplies after four months. She wasn't married. She had no kids, and her home wasn't a B&B. It was almost like she knew this event was going to happen and she'd stocked up ahead of time.

He had to say it was a little disconcerting to know that the town manager was faring better than most in the community and yet she had the nerve to act like she was struggling just as much as anyone else. He had a good mind to blow the whistle on her.

"You still breathing in there, Jake?" Teresa said with a smirk.

"Hilarious," he replied. "Don't worry about me, I haven't eaten this well in months."

"What?" She charged over and flung the door open; a gust of fresh air blew in and he felt his lungs come alive.

"Joking," he said. "Just joking. Your cache of goods are all still here."

She ground her teeth, narrowed her gaze and pointed a finger at him before closing the door before he could say anymore. All the blinds in the kitchen had been closed to prevent anyone from observing from the outside. They wanted to lure them in. The front and rear door had been left unlocked but they had rigged up a small trip wire that was powered by a battery that would cause a red LED light to flash inside the pantry if they entered through the rear, and blue if they came through the front.

Jake had been observing it non-stop, almost willing it to flash so he could get this over with and go home. As much as he was glad to help, he kind of felt bamboozled into being the inside man. He thought he'd be outside, observing from afar, and rush in at the last minute. Hero status without injury. Accolades with reduced risk. Nope. He had front row seats to the show. Like a lamb led to the slaughter. Still, Sam had outfitted him with a ballistic vest, and given him a SIG Sauer P226. Squeezing the grip tightly he rolled his shoulders to work out the tension in his muscles.

Teresa continued to putter around the kitchen. How many mason jars could one person own? For someone that was adamant about not being put in the line of fire, she certainly acted as if the whole thing was a joke. She didn't seem to understand the gravity of the situation.

But she would.

Suddenly, the red light started blinking.

Knowing that the previous victims had been struck on the back of the head, they'd advised Teresa to keep her back turned and stay a good distance away from any of the halls in her home — the same ones that led down to her rear and front door entrances.

Jake's heart started thumping hard.

He wanted to alert Teresa but she would have screamed or done something to jeopardize their one chance. Of course there was also the fact that it could just be Carl or Sam but they'd radio if they were coming in. He reached for his radio to give them the heads-up when he noticed it was turned off. How the hell did that happen? As he switched it on, Sam's voice came over the speaker. "Jake. Jake. Pick up!"

Keeping the volume low and peering out through the slats of the door he answered.

"I hear you. What is it?"

"We've got a breach. They…"

"Already entered," Jake shot back before Sam could finish. "The red light…"

He was in the middle of speaking when a hooded figure came into view carrying a baseball bat. The figure crept up closer to Teresa. She was completely unaware, humming to herself. Jake took a step back and kicked the pantry door while bringing up the gun. "Put it down!" he yelled. Teresa screamed and the figure darted for the corridor. Slipping on the waxed floor, the intruder slammed a shoulder into the wall.

A scramble to escape through the rear exit was cut short by the appearance of Sam, panting and out of breath. "Police. Stop!"

Not missing a beat, the intruder shifted gear and dashed into the living room hoping to make a break for the front door. Jake was already on it, cutting him off through the French doors farther down. He burst through them and launched himself at the figure, slamming into him and landing on a glass coffee table. It smashed beneath them and a struggle ensued for a moment, until Jake pulled back the hood.

"Ian?!"

Shocked but not enough to let him go, Jake held on for dear life as he wrestled to escape. Sam blasted into the room, rifle at the ready, aimed down at him. "Don't even think about it!" he bellowed. Jake turned him towards Sam. "Ian Hudson?"

They didn't know what was more shocking, the fact that it wasn't Mick or that it was a close friend, a family man that he'd been trying to convince to stay at the Manor. He now understood why Ian didn't want to be there. He would have been under the watchful eye of more than just his wife.

When he had been handcuffed, dragged to his feet and thrown onto a sofa, Teresa entered the room, screaming bloody murder.

"Jake. Get her out of here," Sam said.

A job easier said than done. She kicked, and thrashed, cursing at Ian. "How dare you come into my house. How dare you..." Quickly, Jake shoved her outside and told her to wait while they dealt with this. He reentered the house just as Sam peppered Ian with questions.

"I don't get it. Why you? Why them? Why sexually assault them?"

His chin dropped and he didn't answer.

"Tell me!" Sam demanded to know, getting close to him and gripping him by the collar. "Carl better not die, or you will," he said before leaving the room to go check on his partner.

Standing there in front of him, Jake couldn't believe it.

"Mick put you up to this?"

He shook his head no. "Do me a favor, don't tell Tess about this."

Jake scoffed. "You think she won't ask where you've gone when you don't return home?" He paused. "Fuck, Ian! Why? Why would you do this?"

"I…" he went to speak but then trailed off.

"You know what, I don't want to know. You killed three innocent women, violated them and tossed them away like garbage. You deserve to hang for what you did. I have a good mind to hand you over to Mick Bennington and let him give the people the justice they deserve." Jake shook his head. He was beginning to think that perhaps they had pegged Mick unfairly. Maybe public hanging was the only way to deal with violent crime and send a message out to the community.

Sam returned with a battered and bruised partner.

"We'll take it from here. Thanks for your help."

Jake nodded, not taking his eyes off Ian for even a second.

As he walked out into the cool night, he wondered what he would tell Tess. She would be devastated, as would their unborn child. Tess hadn't shared the news with Ian yet but Sara knew. She'd told Jake and had him promise to keep it a secret.

A secret? How many other people in the community of Castine were keeping secrets? How would that affect them, and their survival? If they couldn't trust those closest to them, who could they trust? Jake wiped beads of sweat from his brow and trudged off into the night, feeling a little less safe, and unsure of the future.

Epilogue

The following two weeks on the Appalachian Trail were brutal. They averaged fifteen to twenty-two miles a day and still had months of hiking before them. Landon was starting to think they would never make it home. From Lost Mountain Shelter to Rice Field Shelter was just over ninety-seven miles. Had they not stopped in several towns, and slept each day, they could have reached it faster but with hunger, thirst, and the elements beating them into submission, it had taken longer.

Although they didn't want to enter towns, it was unavoidable after the run-in with the underhanded Terry and Nancy. Landon tried to think of it in a positive light. Sure, they lost the lion's share of their hiking gear but had it not been for them, he was certain that Beth or himself would have died.

It had taken six towns before they managed to collect enough hiking gear from homes and stores that had been broken into in order to continue. It wasn't at the level they had before but it was enough.

A sleeping bag for Beth.

A portable stove.

Additional ammo.

Water purifying equipment.

Canned food.

Matches to make Beth's life easier.

She'd ended up with some gnarly blisters on her hands from using a hand drill which required rolling the wood between the palms until an ember was formed. It was old school but damn he was glad her father had taught her how to do it.

It was actually amazing what could be scavenged from old farmhouses close to the towns. There were thousands of residential homes scattered throughout the country, some lived in, others abandoned and the rest were owned by those who had died.

He wasn't sure how long they would stay at the shelter, as a terrible hailstorm had swept in and bombed the earth with bullet-size ice pellets for the past hour. Using the situation to their advantage, they decided to take the time to eat and rest.

The shelter was nestled in the woods on three sides and exposed to an open field at the front of the shelter. Landon looked out thoughtfully as hail battered the ground. He scooped warm soup into his mouth and relished the taste. They'd got lucky at a house not far from there. The owners had left a pantry half full of canned food and pickled goods. At first, they were confused as to why they didn't take it with them, but that was soon answered when Beth found their bodies hanging from the rafters in the barn. It was a sad fact but some people weren't strong enough to deal with the new world. Fear of hunger. Fear of attack. Fear of the unknown was too much for many. They'd gathered as much as they could carry and left quickly just in case trouble showed up.

"Didn't your father buy canned food?" He asked.

"Not often. We caught our meat, grew our vegetables

and my mother made bread. Butter, eggs and milk came from the animals we had."

"And you didn't miss it?"

"How can you miss what you never had?"

He cocked his head. "Good point." He stopped eating and tossed his plastic spoon in the bowl. "You know, I once tried to give up Starbucks."

She chuckled. "Oh yeah, how did that go?"

"I did it. Made it nine months until I got a headache I couldn't kick. Three days that migraine kicked my ass." He nodded slowly. "Anyway I knew that one cup of java from that store would nip it in the bud."

"Did it work?"

"Hell yeah."

"Did you continue drinking it?"

He snorted. "Yeah, that was eight years ago. Right up until the blackout I was hooked on it like an addict."

"I'm not sure what is sadder, that you got hooked on coffee again, or that you willingly paid exorbitant prices for a cup of coffee that you could have made for a fraction of the price from home."

He nodded in agreement. "Trust me. Sara thought I was nuts going out buying from them every day. But..." he trailed off, his brow furrowing.

"What is it?"

"You hear that?" Landon asked.

"Hear what? All I hear is the hail."

"I must be going mad." He returned to tucking into his food when he heard it again. A scream. Landon rose from a cross-legged position and went to the mouth of the shelter. He cocked his head.

"Landon. It's just your mind playing tricks," Beth said. "Happens all the time in the woods. It's probably just—"

A yell for help cut through the steady battering of ice pellets. Landon dropped his bowl and scooped up his rifle, launching himself out into the howling wind, heading in the direction he heard it. Beth yelled. "Hold up, Landon." His feet pounded the earth as the rain soaked him, and pellets stung his skin.

The yelling got louder the closer he got.

Drenched, he slalomed around trees scanning the terrain, looking for any sign of life. Nothing. Then the cry came again, just over the rise. Landon made it to the top just in time to see two men fighting in a clearing. Both were covered in blood, they were rolling in the mud, one of them holding a knife above the other.

"Drop it!" Landon bellowed, his gun raised at the man on top.

"You don't understand."

"Put it down."

"I can't."

Landon hunched forward; his eyes focused on the one on top who looked intent on killing the one beneath. Their skin was covered in blood and mud, their clothes matted and drenched. "Toss the knife."

"No. He killed the members of my camp."

The muddied man below him shot back. "Bullshit. He's lying. He killed my friends. Shoot him."

By now Beth had caught up, with Grizzly in tow.

Landon pressed forward closing the distance. "Throw

the knife!"

"I can't do it. I won't."

"Shoot him!" the guy yelled beneath.

"Put it down. Don't make me do it."

The one on top was no longer listening. He reared back his arm about to slice when Landon squeezed a round that hit him in the shoulder. The man dropped to one side but it didn't stop him. A momentary cry of pain and he scrambled forward for another attack. Landon had no choice. He squeezed another round, this one lanced through his skull, dropping him in an instant.

Silence, except for hail.

The man on the ground froze, staring back at Landon. "Thank you. Thank you," he said scrambling away from the corpse looking scared. Landon shifted the gun toward him.

He threw hands up. "Whoa! You can lower that now. I was telling the truth."

"What happened?" Landon asked.

"We met him on the trail, a group of us were camping

about a mile from here. He must have been on drugs or something as he just attacked us. Killed three of my friends before chasing me. If you hadn't shot him, he would have killed me."

Grizzly growled and Beth noted his reaction.

"What are you doing out here?" Beth asked.

"Hiking. Surviving. You?"

"Same. Heading for Maine."

"Huh. That's where I'm going. I mean, where we were heading."

The man wiped mud from his face with the back of his arm which was equally caked up. He pulled at his shoulder-length hair. "Man, I could kill for a cigarette. You wouldn't have one, would you?"

It struck Landon as a strange request but then again, in times of stress cigarettes had been the one thing he'd reached for. It was the reason why he had struggled to quit. Landon studied him for a second then reached into his jacket. "Strangely enough, I do. An entire packet, minus one. Was about the only thing that survived the trip," he said removing the crumpled packet. "Don't have a light but you're welcome to them," he said, tossing the packet.

"That's kind of you," the man replied, catching them. "Maybe I can go with you. Safety in numbers and whatnot," he said. His eyes darted between them as if waiting for a response. Landon looked at Beth to gauge her reaction. She shrugged.

"I guess we could use the company," Landon said.

"Cool. Okay." He panted hard and turned towards the trail. "You at the shelter nearby?"

Landon nodded.

"I'll meet you there."

"Where you heading now?" Landon asked.

"To get my gear — and my banjo."

"Banjo?"

"Yeah," he said with a smile as he scooped up the knife and tucked it into his waistband. He pulled back his long hippie hair and used a small black hair tie from his pocket to get it out of his face.

Landon frowned. "What's your name?"

"Billy. But most call me Maestro."

In the hailing storm, they watched the strange man amble away, grateful for their help, promising to return with additional supplies. Grizzly let out another low growl and Beth patted him on the head. "It's okay, boy, it's okay. It's over."

But it wasn't over. They still had over a thousand miles to go before they reached Mount Katahdin in Maine, and more before he would see Sara and Max again. Now they had company, whether that was a blessing or a curse was unknown.

But come hell or high water, nothing and no one would come between him and home.

* * *

THANK YOU FOR READING

Book #3 All That Escapes will be out soon

Please consider leaving a review. Even a few words is really appreciated. Thanks kindly, Jack.

About the Author

Jack Hunt is the International Bestselling Author of horror, sci-fi and post-apocalyptic novels. He currently has over forty books published. Jack lives on the East coast of North America. If you haven't joined Jack Hunt's Private Facebook Group you can request to join by going here.

https://www.facebook.com/groups/1620726054688731/

This gives readers a way to chat with Jack, see cover reveals, and stay updated on upcoming releases. There is also his main Facebook page if you want to browse that.

www.jackhuntbooks.com

jhuntauthor@gmail.com

CPSIA information can be obtained
at www.ICGtesting.com
Printed in the USA
BVHW030230010921
615779BV00006B/207